Book #4

M000289057

Washed Up

Laurinda Wallace

Laurinda Wallace

Cover Design by Annie Moril

Back Cover Photo by Laurinda Wallace

Author Photo by Reign Photography

ALL RIGHTS RESERVED

No part of this publication may be reproduced, stored in a retrieval system, or transmitted, in any form or by any means-electronic, mechanical, photocopying, recording, or otherwise-without prior written permission.

This is a work of fiction. Any references to real events, businesses, organizations, and locales are intended only to give the fiction a sense of reality and authenticity. Any resemblance to actual persons, living or dead is coincidental.

Copyright © 2016 Laurinda Wallace

All rights reserved.

ISBN: 10-0692626948

ISBN-13: 978-0692626948

DEDICATION

To the memory of Clancy—a great dog and faithful companion. A top-class Labrador Retriever.

2002 - 2015

ACKNOWLEDGMENTS

The mystique of the Wild West is steeped in the wonderful place I now call home. The Huachuca Mountains, the San Pedro River, Tombstone, Bisbee, and most of all the people who live here, make Cochise County one of the best places you'll find to live and work.

Its colorful history only adds to the intrigue and charm of the Land of Legends. Who hasn't heard the tales of Geronimo, Cochise, Wyatt Earp, Doc Holliday, or Ike Clanton? While little mining and cattle ranching still remain, the high desert today is where cutting-edge technology is developed and vineyards produce award winning wine. The diverse wildlife, sky island ecosystems, and world-class birding makes southeastern Arizona a place for all sorts of adventures.

CHAPTER 1

Coronado National Forest, Hereford, AZ

The half-submerged body in the mountain stream confirmed Gracie's misgivings about the timing of her vacation. She stumbled backward into Amanda Littlefield, turning away from the disfigured remains of the man sloshing against the bank of the stream that a few minutes ago had been touted as a pleasant rest stop. Amanda stifled a scream and clutched Gracie's arm.

"Oh, no," Amanda cried, twisting to dig into her backpack, finally fishing out a cell phone. "I'd better ..."

The plump, middle-aged woman's knees buckled, and Gracie caught her B & B hostess. She eased Amanda to the ground, steering her away from the grisly sight.

"Don't look," Gracie warned. "And take some deep breaths, head down."

Amanda complied and pulled the backpack off, locating her water bottle. She gulped the liquid and took a couple of deep breaths before making the phone call.

"Gary, this is Amanda. I need some help. I just found ... found a body at Miner's Springs. I'm not sure ..."

The woman rose and walked unsteadily toward a pinkish-gray boulder and leaned against it, the cell phone still to her ear.

"I'm at the springs right now. We need help."

Gracie joined the shaken woman, feeling a little unsteady herself.

"Are they coming?"

"It'll be a few minutes. There are a couple of Border Patrol agents up there looking for illegals, so Gary's bringing them too. How could this have happened?"

Gracie cringed, looking over Amanda's shoulder at the battered body of a man, lying face up. The head and torso were partially submerged, his left leg wedged between two larger rocks. His hiking boot dangled above the water, a dragonfly resting on the toe.

Sitting down next to Amanda, she tried to distract herself by admiring the waterfalls that spilled prettily into the pool holding the body, before the stream pushed through some large boulders that rimmed the banks. Then it seemed to disappear among a pile of smaller rocks and a layer of dead leaves.

She'd been excited to explore the Huachuca Mountains with Amanda this morning, who was eager to introduce her guest to the unique "sky island" forested terrain in the high desert of southeastern Arizona. Already, her expectation of sand and cactus had been pleasantly replaced with the lush grasslands in the valley and the thickly forested mountains that surrounded the B & B. There were plenty of prickly pears and other cactus varieties, but not the thorny landscape she'd imagined.

Taking a deep breath, her racing heart slowed and her wobbly legs stabilized. The sound of tromping feet obliged Gracie to look up. Two men in green uniforms hustled down the steep incline. One was already on a cell phone. She gave them a tight smile as they strode to the water and bent to check the body. One of the agents shook his head at his partner, dropping the lifeless arm back into the water. Amanda thrust her hands in the pockets of her jeans and backed away. Pounding of more feet caught Gracie's attention. She looked up to see two men in T-shirts and jeans kicking up dust in their descent. It was probably the trail maintenance team. She and Amanda should be helping repair a section of washed-out trail somewhere above the waterfalls. She'd expected to shore up part of a switchback, not discover the remains of a stranger. A gray-haired, leanly built African-American man went directly to Amanda, while the other stopped and looked at the scene below.

"Gary," Amanda called out.

The man's eyes widened in what Gracie suspected was recognition when he stared at the lifeless form, lying in the water.

"Ohh ..." Gary groaned. "I ... I hate to say this, but it looks like Manny. He wasn't answering his phone."

Amanda nodded in agreement. "It's gotta be Manny. I recognize the shirt and the hiking boots."

"Hey, everybody, stay up above," the taller of the Border Patrol agents instructed them. We don't want the scene contaminated."

The agent motioned for them to join a yet unidentified man who stood on the upper trail. Amanda quickly joined the man, Gary on her heels. Gracie kept her distance, suddenly feeling like a fifth wheel and not sure what she should do next.

"Gracie. Come on over. We could be here a while," Amanda called to her.

The men shifted to look at Gracie. Faces were grim, but both managed to offer wan smiles.

"This is Gracie Andersen," said Amanda. "She's a guest at the ranch, hailing from back east. Not exactly what I expected to find when I dragged her up here this morning."

Amanda jabbed a thumb at the men. "Hank and Gary." Gracie returned the stiff greetings, studying the agents who now stood talking on the bank below.

The group began to settle in for a long wait on law enforcement. Gracie took the cue and found a small boulder with enough flat surface to provide a seat. The statement by the Border Patrol agent suddenly hit her. She turned to Amanda, who wedged herself in next to her.

"Do they think it's a crime scene? What did he mean by 'we don't want the scene contaminated'?"

The gray-haired woman shrugged, her lips pressed tightly together. Amanda slid off her perch to join Gary, who stood watching the agents. The air smelled of dust, charred wood, and the spicy juniper that dotted the mountainside. Two large sycamores shaded the stream, and then a break in the trees offered Gracie a glimpse of the San Pedro River valley. She wished she could truly enjoy the view, but her stomach remained unsettled from the ugly discovery in the water.

"Gracie, I'm Hank Ramage," the dark-haired, lightly bearded man stepped forward and extended a hand to her. "This is a terrible thing to happen up here today. Gary's right. I think it must be Manny. Probably had a heart attack. I know he was seeing the doctor quite a bit lately." He took off a worn cowboy hat, wiping sweat with a dirty bandanna from his pocket.

"A heart attack?" Gracie blurted out.

Hank's face reddened, and he began to knock dust off his jeans before sitting down on a gnarled stump.

She was confused. Her first impression had been that the man had probably fallen from the overhang above the water or maybe someone had helped him over the edge since the Border Patrol agents wanted to preserve the scene. Maybe they were being extra cautious. But then, maybe the guy had a heart attack above the water and fell over the cliff. She may have been hasty in her assessment of the man's observation.

Gracie shifted uneasily, looking for another conversation starter. "Does he ... Manny have family?"

Hank turned back, his features more composed. "Yeah. He's got a couple of adult sons. They work for the government somewhere in back east. He and his wife took in a foster kid a few months ago. Manny's been trying to get

4

him straightened out."

"Oh," Gracie said slowly.

Scattering stones and heavy footsteps from the trail above announced the arrival of a brown-uniformed man who appeared from behind some large boulders flanking the trail.

"Hey, Armando!" Hank called.

"What's happening here?" Armando asked.

According to the patch on his shirt, Armando Ortiz was a Park Service ranger. He removed a cap, wiping sweat from his forehead with the back of his hand. His black hair was cropped close to his head, his features topped with heavy eyebrows. His physique bespoke of regular weight lifting.

Gary stepped forward, putting a hand on the ranger's shoulder. "I'm pretty sure we've found Manny. It's bad." He nodded his head toward the water below.

"What?"

The ranger twisted away from Gary, making short work of the distance between him and the Border Patrol agents.

The distant rumble of thunder and a sudden whoosh of wind turned everyone's attention to the darkening sky. Gary shook his head and rubbed his hands together.

"We don't want to be caught in a storm up here. Maybe we should at least get back to the trailhead," he suggested.

"I'm with you. Let me ask Armando," Hank offered, already starting the descent to the stream.

The ranger waved him back and joined the uneasy group. He pulled a small notebook from his breast pocket. "Did anyone hear anything this morning? Yelling? Anything unusual?"

"No. Nothing out of the ordinary," Gary responded. "Anybody else hear something?"

"Not a thing," Amanda said.

"I didn't either," Hank confirmed. "We were digging out the trail and shoring it up where the rains had washed it out." He scuffed the ground with his hiking boot. "Manny was supposed to meet us by 7:30, but never showed."

"Do you think he lost his balance and fell?" Amanda

asked.

"I really don't know, Amanda. I'm not even sure it's Manny. That'll be something for the medical examiner to figure out." The ranger glanced over at Gracie. "I know everybody else here, but you. Can I get your name, miss?"

"Gracie Andersen. I'm staying at Amanda's B & B."

He scribbled the information into the notebook and tucked it into his pocket.

"What about us getting out of here before that storm comes in?" Gary asked. "We're due for some real rain."

The ranger considered the request, glancing back at the Border Patrol agents standing at the water's edge with the body.

"I guess that's all right. I've got everybody's contact information." He rubbed his jaw, still considering. "Yeah. Go ahead."

One of the Border Patrol agents yelled, "Hey!" motioning Ortiz back to the pool. After a brief conversation, the park ranger returned to the group.

"On second thought, Agent Carlisle will escort you to the parking lot. There'll be formal statements needed. It looks like we've got a suspicious death here."

It was exactly what Gracie didn't want to hear. This could ruin a perfectly nice vacation.

The hike back to the parking lot was much quicker and less taxing than the ascent. Gracie easily kept pace with the experienced group, which was gratifying after lagging behind her older hostess on the climb. Two black SUVs with U.S. government plates and an ambulance were in the trailhead's parking lot. A crew of EMTs carrying a foldup stretcher were about to tackle the switchback. Taking a swig from her almost empty water bottle, Gracie watched four men in identical polo shirts exit the SUVs and join the ambulance crew on the trail.

A breeze fluttered through the trees, followed within seconds by thunder. Glad for the safety of Amanda's beat-up Ford pickup, Gracie slammed the door against the approaching storm.

What kind of dumb luck was it to stumble onto a dead body in the first few days of a long-awaited vacation? Marc, no doubt, would be pleased as punch to find her in the middle of another suspicious death investigation. At least she had absolutely no ties to whoever was in the water. She couldn't possibly know any suspects either. She had her fingers crossed that it was an accidental fall or even a heart attack that would get her out of a witness situation with Arizona law enforcement. However, the condition of the body left plenty of room for foul play, and the agents must have seen something to confirm that.

Two Cochise County deputies met them in the parking lot and began taking their statements. She was the only one of the four who didn't know Manny, and her interview was mercifully short. Her driver's license, her vacation plans, and a description of the scene were recorded quickly. Amanda's interview was finished before Gary's and Hank's. Amanda, looking pale and shaky, headed for her pickup.

"Do you want me to drive?" Gracie asked.

Amanda's eyes were a little weepy, and she grasped the steering wheel so that her knuckles were white.

"No. Thanks though. I'm really sorry, Gracie. Really sorry."

"Don't worry about it. I'm sorry about your friend ... if it's really him. Maybe it's not and he ..."

Amanda shook her head. "It's Manny. I'd bet money on it."

She started the engine and pulled out onto the highway.

"That rain looks like it's coming soon," Gracie remarked, trying to change the subject.

Thunderheads shadowed the Huachucas, and she thought she'd spotted a couple of flashes of lightning. She didn't envy the men navigating a body in a litter down the mountain. Hopefully they'd make it before any serious rain fell.

"It's hard to tell where it'll rain down here in the valley, but the mountains are going to really get nailed." Amanda seemed to be reading Gracie's thoughts. "I sure hope they get him off the mountain before it cuts loose."

Gracie nodded and sighed. A beep from her phone alerted her to a text. She swiped the screen and read, "Meeting you at the ranch. Are you all right?"

Word sure traveled fast in law enforcement.

***

Marc's truck was in the B & B's parking lot. He was scratching the heads of the resident border collie and a three-legged Rhodesian ridgeback, Molly and Cochise respectively, who were the designated greeters. Cochise had tangled with a rattlesnake as a pup and lost his leg to the nasty venom. He was undeterred from patrolling the grounds and kept an eye out for hawks and coyotes. Amanda kept a small barn-red henhouse, with a flock of Rhode Island reds and Americanas in a wire enclosure. He was their personal security guard, keeping aerial and terrestrial intruders away. Gracie thoroughly enjoyed watching his methodical circuit every morning, the missing left hind leg apparently of no consequence.

Molly landed in Gracie's lap as soon as she opened the door.

"Hey there, girl!" Gracie laughed as the dog licked her face.

The black and white dog had formed an instant bond with her on day one, which was nice since Gracie was fiercely missing her black Lab, Haley.

"Molly, get out of here," Amanda bellowed.

The dog scampered away, feathery tail waving all the way to the front door.

Marc met the women on the gravel walkway to the huge Santa Fe style house, which was the main gathering place for breakfast. It also contained Amanda's living quarters. Large wooden timbers jutted from the sand-colored stucco exterior, just below the flat roofline, which was composed of one large and two smaller square sections. A wide porch area with a tiled roof welcomed guests at the entrance. The front doors opened into a bright, blue and yellow-tiled foyer.

A double set of patio doors opened into a courtyard filled with flowers and hummingbird feeders.

"Are you two okay?" he asked as they entered the foyer.

"A little shook up, but we're all right," Gracie answered. "You sure found out quick enough."

"One of the agents you met up there knows me. He called after you identified yourself. I guess I've mentioned your name a few times." He smiled and put an arm around Gracie's shoulder.

"Is that right?" She returned the smile and settled in closer.

"I still can't believe Manny is dead," Amanda declared, her voice cracking with emotion.

"I'm sorry, Amanda," Marc said. "It's pretty gruesome to find a friend that way."

"Sorry. Please excuse me," Amanda croaked, heading for the entrance to her private living area.

Gracie and Marc mumbled apologies and relocated to the courtyard. The dogs appeared and flopped into the shade of some tall flowers that were unfamiliar to Gracie. The orange and pink-sherbet-colored spikes of tubular blooms were clustered at the edge of the walkway providing convenient shade for the dogs that panted heavily in the heat. Several tables for two placed throughout the courtyard allowed easy viewing of the feeders. Bright-colored hummers darted between the feeders, buzzing their displeasure at any interlopers who hogged their nectar. Blue salvias and red yucca with jagged, knife-sharp leaves enticed the little nectar sippers, leading to combative territorial disputes. Even with the shade, the air was sizzling. A dry heat was still hot, Gracie decided.

"I feel kind of weird staying here after this has happened," Gracie began.

"Amanda will regroup. She's got other guests besides you to take care of," Marc quickly replied. "Lupita is right here to help out too."

"I know. It's just that it was gruesome. The body that is." Gracie shuddered and leaned forward, elbows on the table. "The man was beaten or maybe fell a ways."

"I'm sorry you had to see that."

"Me too. But something the agents saw sure made them believe his death is suspicious."

"How about a distraction to take your mind off this morning's event?"

"Are you finally off duty? If you are, I'd like to explore Bisbee."

"Sure. Bisbee is always interesting. Let's get some lunch there. I know a great little place in Old Bisbee I think you'll like."

***

Gracie was instantly enamored with the old mining town precariously constructed into the side of rugged, reddish-colored mountains. Narrow streets, long stairways that led to tiny, colorful houses high above the section called Old Bisbee made her feel like she'd stepped back in time. Her nighttime reading of a couple of historical booklets in her casita had already filled her in on the copper mining, which boomed at the turn of the 20th century. Bisbee was the county seat, usurping Tombstone's role in 1929. Refusing to turn the lights out when the copper mines closed in 1975, Bisbee became a tourist destination with restaurants, galleries, and antique shops filling storefronts along the main street.

The smell of roasting coffee from Peddler's Alley drew Marc and Gracie in for a perfectly brewed cup of Ethiopian java before they walked toward the regal Copper Queen Hotel overlooking the downtown area. Marc promised her an authentic Mexican lunch at Santiago's situated below the hotel on Brewery Gulch. A clap of thunder turned their gaze to the imminent storm pushing over the Mule Mountains into town. Marc grabbed Gracie's hand and they dashed down the busy sidewalks, dodging shoppers also headed for shelter from the large raindrops. It began to pour the minute they charged through the doors of the restaurant. Fortunately, they'd escaped the deluge. Within minutes, the monsoon rain flooded the streets, while they munched on homemade salsa and tortilla chips. As suddenly as the rain had gushed from the skies, it stopped.

Gracie took a second bite of a luscious chimichanga when Marc received a text. His presence was immediately required in Sierra Vista, which was 30 minutes away. He and Max, his German shepherd, were needed to find a missing teenager. Disappointment and a simmering anger threatened to become verbalized. Gracie intentionally took another quick bite of the crispy tortilla filled with well-seasoned beef and beans to prohibit the utterance of a regrettable comment. The list of reasons why she should have stayed in Deer Creek grew again. She'd barely seen Marc since her arrival. He was completely immersed in investigating an important drug case. Apparently, they couldn't enjoy a meal together, even though he was officially off duty. So much for an intimate lunch.

CHAPTER 2

Max and Marc joined the search-and-rescue team that was ready to tackle Ash Canyon. The rain had stopped in the mountains, and the smell of damp earth permeated the air. Max whined and pulled against the thick leather leash.

"Settle down, Max," Marc commanded. "We'll be going in a minute."

Sergeant Craig Ames, lanky with wheat-colored hair, slung a camo pack over his shoulder. "Hey, Marc. Nice dog. Does he have a lot of experience in the field?"

"No, Sergeant. This is only his second time out for this. We're getting ready for El Paso. Just waiting for the paperwork."

"Good. Well, we need all hands on deck today. Got a 17-year-old possible runaway that's involved in drugs. A friend of his was pulled out of the canyon a little while ago. He wasn't in real good shape, and we airlifted him to Tucson. Broken arm and a back injury. Kid was a little shocky. He told us that this Ricky Fuentes had taken off and left him. No answer on Fuentes's cell phone. It's either off or the battery died. He may have stolen the Explorer over there." The deputy pointed toward a parking lot on the opposite side of the road. A maroon-colored SUV sat on the far side of the parking area. "They're trying to get a hold of the owners to see if they're hiking up here or missing a vehicle."

"Any idea where Fuentes was headed?" Marc asked. He checked the top on his canteen before clipping it to his belt.

"Not sure, but they got into a disagreement for some reason. Could be a drug deal gone bad. This Fuentes kid has some history with cocaine. We can't even be sure he's still up here. He could've gotten a ride pretty easily." The sergeant sighed, shaking his head. "I won't ever understand this crazy drug stuff."

"Me neither. What about the kid's parents?"

"No go. Fuentes was taken from his biological parents a few months ago. We think the SUV actually belongs to his foster parents. Miguel, the kid we found—his parents called in a missing person report this morning. Never came home from school yesterday. They were out looking for him all night. He's never been in trouble, but when we heard he was with the Fuentes kid ... well, that wasn't a good sign. Miguel managed to call his parents for help a couple of hours ago, and we were lucky to find him." The man twisted around to check on the team's progress. "Everybody ready to move out?"

***

Gracie perched on a stool in the ranch's kitchen, sipping an iced coffee. Amanda finished unloading the dishwasher and leaned against the counter.

"So, you and Marc are serious?"

Gracie chuckled glumly. Amanda certainly didn't beat around the bush.

"Supposedly. This trip was really his idea, but so far, he's been pretty tied up with his temporary job here. I guess that's law enforcement though."

"Or the military. My husband and I have been apart more than we've been together for 30 years. He's retiring at the end of September. Frankly, I'm not sure about us actually living together—all the time, that is."

"You'll figure it out."

"I'm not sure I'd put money on it myself. This ranch was my idea, and Cal's not real keen on running a business like this in retirement. I think he'd rather be on a beach in

Belize or Panama."

"He's not a fan of the West?"

"Cal likes it well enough." Amanda paused. "Let's say we've got some things to work out when he comes home for good."

"Sounds like where Marc and I are at. I thought our relationship was over when he took this little six-month transfer to Arizona. However, the separation actually was a good thing. If we ever have some solid time together, we might figure out our relationship, and where it's headed. His job is more time-consuming than I understood, and that scares me."

"Marc says a lot of good things about you. I'm sure it'll be fine." Amanda watched two couples leave the parking area and head for the path that led to the guest casitas. She turned back to Gracie.

"You're an independent businesswoman. You make decisions every day. You're in charge of your own destiny."

Gracie's brow wrinkled, trying to decipher Amanda's drift. It seemed the woman was talking more about herself than Gracie.

"Right. But I have a partner and a lot of responsibilities too."

Her phone chirped with a text notification. She hoped it was Marc telling her the search-and-rescue team had found the missing boy so they could do some more sightseeing. Glancing at the phone display, she saw Jim Taylor's name, her business partner. She needed to call the kennel. Excusing herself, she found a comfortable seat in the reading room off the foyer.

"Hey, Chief," was Jim's warm greeting.

"What's going on?"

"Sorry to bother you again, but we've got a situation here."

"What kind of situation?"

"It's the reservation software. It crashed."

"What? You're kidding! What happened?"

"Cheryl can't get it to work at all. The system went

down last night right before closing. I told her to shut down the computer and try again this morning. She's been working on it all day."

"Is she there? I can try to walk her through a restart."

"Uh … no. It's past closing time now."

Gracie looked at her watch. She kept forgetting about the three-hour time difference. It was already six in Deer Creek. Why hadn't he called her earlier?

"I can try to walk you through it then. You should've called me sooner."

"I did. You didn't answer." Jim's voice had a distinct edge to it.

She hadn't checked her phone since the discovery of the body that morning. In fact, she now remembered turning it off when the park ranger had taken her initial statement.

"Sorry. I turned off my phone earlier. Well, we need to get this fixed. There's a folder with the company's contact info in my bottom drawer. They should be able to help."

"Already called them. Apparently, the company is being bought out. Customer service isn't that helpful right now."

Gracie made a fist and pounded her forehead. This was not a problem to have in the middle of summer vacations. Milky Way Kennels was booked almost completely through August. The software took care of all the scheduling of reservations and grooming appointments for the business.

All right," she groaned, closing her eyes.

The problem had happened once before. Maybe she could remember the process that customer service had given her over a year ago. "Are you near the computer?"

***

Amanda looked up to see her chef and assistant manager, Lupita Alvarez, enter through the side door to the large kitchen. She lugged a box of fresh produce, which she dumped into the sink. Gracie's voice rose in volume, making it impossible for the two women to ignore. Lupita placed large poblano peppers and sweet onions on a cutting board.

"Miss Gracie seems pretty upset." Lupita wiped her hands on a small towel.

"The joys of running your own business," Amanda replied, reaching into the refrigerator for a can of Sprite.

"Like those two staying in casita *nueve*?" Lupita sliced into an onion with large chef's knife.

Amanda frowned. "Exactly. Have they been around today?"

"No. They asked for an early breakfast, remember?"

"Now I do. They must have gone back to explore Coronado again today. I saw their Jeep at the trailhead parking lot."

"They said they were going back up there." Lupita snapped the lids shut on the plastic containers of chopped vegetables. "The blond one ... Alex had an old map he was studying with Justin." Her Spanish accent softened the "J."

Amanda huffed. "Those idiots won't find any treasure up there. They're trying to score a TV reality show. They might as well try to find the Lost Dutchman's Mine as Coronado's treasure."

Lupita laughed. "They seem pretty sure of themselves."

"Of course, they are. They're young and full of testosterone-fueled egos. Ida didn't find any more tequila bottles lying outside their casita, did she?"

"No. But there was a certain weedy smell in the casita when she cleaned today."

"Excellent! I'll probably have more complaints about them. When do they leave?"

"I don't remember." Lupita took off her apron, hanging it on a wall hook on the back of the walk-in pantry door.

Amanda pulled the reservation book from a desk drawer. "Ah ... yes." She ran her finger down the appropriate page. "Saturday morning, is it? Good! I have a family coming that afternoon that will need the casita because of the two bedrooms. *Adios* to our treasure hunters then."

Gracie's sudden presence in the kitchen interrupted Amanda's next comment.

"Everything all right?" Amanda asked her.

"Keeping my fingers crossed. A software issue, but it's working for the time being." Gracie rubbed the back of her neck. "This was supposed to be a vacation, but I feel like I've spent more time on the phone fixing problems at the kennel than relaxing. Of course, Marc hasn't been around that much either. It's been mostly frustrating."

"Don't worry, Miss Gracie," Lupita soothed. "Let me get you something to eat."

"No thanks, Lupita. Marc just texted me. With any luck, he'll be here to pick me up in an hour. We're going to Pizzeria Mimosa for dinner tonight."

"*Bueno*! You wait. Everything will be okay," Lupita assured her. "I have to go. I'll be here at 6:30 tomorrow, Señora."

"Thanks for staying later, Lupita," Amanda said. "You were a lifesaver today."

Lupita waved and slipped out through the courtyard.

"So, he's finished with the search and rescue?" Amanda tossed the soda can in the garbage.

"He and Max are done for the day. Max cut a pad pretty deeply. Marc had to actually carry him for about a mile."

"Whoa! He's a big dog. I hope he'll be all right—Max, that is."

"I think so. Marc was able to find a vet to stitch him up."

"Did they find whoever was lost?"

"One was found and taken to Tucson. The other boy is still missing."

"Any names? Are they local?"

"Marc didn't tell me the name of the teenager they found, but the one still missing is Ricky Fuentes."

Amanda's face blanched, and she swallowed hard.

"What's the matter?" Gracie asked.

"You're sure it's Ricky Fuentes?"

"Yes. Why?"

"He's Manny's foster kid.".

CHAPTER 3

Gracie settled herself in the courtyard to watch black-chinned and rufous hummingbirds dive-bomb each other, while Marc made a series of phone calls about the missing teenager's connection to the late Manny. Plenty of officers appeared to be working on the case at this point. Marc's inability to stand down and relax was becoming more than a little aggravating. Marc flashed a smile at Gracie when a copper and green colored rufous buzzed past his head.

"Those little things are aggressive," he commented, laying the phone on the table.

"Did they find that kid?" Gracie asked.

"No sign of him yet. If he's hurt, it won't be good to be out on the mountain all night."

Gracie shivered, thinking of the wildlife that might be interested in an injured teen. "Let's hope they find him before dark."

"Yeah," Marc responded absently. His eyes were not on her but directed at the splashing fountain. "There's an all-out manhunt for him now. He probably stole the victim's vehicle. Those boys may be involved with his death."

"That's terrible. But no one heard anything along the trail this morning. We didn't see or hear anything out of the ordinary when we were hiking. Neither did anybody else. At least that's what they said."

Her stomach growled, reminding her that Italian cuisine had been promised. She wondered if he was ever going to suggest that they get some dinner.

As if on cue, Marc turned back to her, with blue eyes twinkling and a smile that made her feel like a melting frozen custard in a waffle cone. "Are you ready to go eat?"

"Absolutely," she replied. "Lead the way."

***

They found seats on the back patio of the restaurant that afforded unobstructed views of the mountains. Mesmerized by the pinks and oranges that streaked the western sky, she missed the server's question the first time.

"Gracie? Do you want something other than water to drink?" Marc asked.

"Oh. Sorry. I'll try an Italian soda—raspberry." She focused her attention on the menu and placed her order.

Marc leaned forward and took the menu from her, handing it to the harried, curly-haired waiter.

"Gracie, I want to apologize for how your vacation has gone. The drug case that I've been working on is suddenly hot and heavy. I talked with the lieutenant today. It's going to be tough to do everything I want to do while you're here. I'm really sorry. Every chance I can, I'll break away. We'll squeeze in some fun, I promise."

Gracie looked into his earnest and enticing eyes, feeling like things might be taking a turn for the better. She knew he was really trying to make everything work.

"That's great. I was beginning to think that my timing was horrible."

"No. Crime has bad timing. The drug cartels are a challenge. It's a complex case that we finally got a break on this week. The missing kids appear to be part of the case. However, the DEA gave us some extra manpower today, so I'm officially at your disposal tonight. No calls and hurried lunches like today." He settled back against the chair. "So, what do you think of Arizona?"

"It's beautiful, but way different from Deer Creek. The mountains are unbelievable." She looked back toward the highest mountain in the range. The sun had almost disappeared, shadows filling the canyons to the foothills. The air was definitely cooler and she took a deep breath, enjoying the lingering scent of rain.

Marc smiled, resting his arm on the table. "I feel the same about the mountains. Max and I have worked in several different areas in the county. Each one has its own beauty. But the woman across the table from me is the real beauty."

Gracie felt her face flush. "Why thank you, sir."

"I know we've had a rocky start all the way around, but I really want to talk to you about where we're headed," Marc said.

"Rocky describes it well," she agreed.

This was a conversation that she was desperate to have and dreaded to some extent. For all the conversations they'd had on Face Time before the trip and her confidence that she was ready for a serious relationship, Gracie's few days of vacation had her back on the fence. Smiling, Gracie brushed back a tendril of auburn hair that the warm evening breeze nudged across her eyes.

"I was looking at this trip as a fresh start to figure out where we're going—if anywhere."

Marc's eyes flickered with concern. "I hope we're going somewhere. This is the place for making a new life. It's big out here—you can be absolutely independent. I can feel it." He made a sweeping gesture with his arm toward the mountains. "It's been that way for me so far. I didn't realize what a rut I was in back in New York. The opportunities in law enforcement here are outstanding, and I'm considering a change myself. Once Max and I are trained in El Paso, I think there's a good possibility that this could be home."

Gracie gasped. "You don't want to come back to Wyoming County?"

She pushed back from the table, her stomach flip-flopping. "I don't understand. The Arizona assignment was a temporary thing. You mentioned the drug dog training in Texas, but somehow I missed the 'not coming back to New

York' part."

The server appeared with hot bread and an antipasto tray. Gracie pulled the small loaf apart, dipping a piece into a dish of olive oil. The smell of fresh bread made her suddenly ravenous.

"That's what I want to explain." Marc popped a small mozzarella ball into his mouth. "You talked a lot about your new life without Michael. How you felt your family was too close—that everything was too much the same."

Her brows furrowed, remembering the most recent conversation with Marc. She had been on a bit of a rant about her family and everyone in town knowing about her personal life. Then there was Isabelle, her thorn-in-the-side cousin, who kept her on her toes. Whether it was a painful social function or wildly concocted gossip, Izzy made living in Deer Creek a misery some days.

A couple followed a hostess to a nearby table. The woman's animated conversation with her date, made the stack of silver bracelets on her slender arm jangle like wind chimes as they passed. Gracie glanced at the man when he sat down. It was Hank Ramage. He smiled in recognition, showing white even teeth.

"Hi ... Gracie. Right?" He rose from his chair.

She made quick introductions, and Hank turned to introduce his girlfriend, Mistee Olin. She was waifish with fine features, long black hair, and red highlights in her bangs.

"Gracie's staying at Amanda's," Hank explained.

"How nice! I'm the massage therapist and yoga instructor on Tuesdays and Thursdays. I haven't seen you at any classes," Mistee twittered.

"Amanda's had me busy with other things," Gracie replied. "Although I've been thinking about scheduling a hot rock massage."

"That's so good for you, but I'd recommend ..." She stopped when Hank touched her arm.

"We'll let you two get back to your conversation." Hank gently steered Mistee back to their table.

Marc frowned and stared over Gracie's shoulder at the parking lot. The silence lengthened between them. She folded and unfolded her napkin, finally smoothing it across her lap.

"Where were we?" She smiled, trying to catch his eye.

Marc's gaze returned to her, and he gave her a lopsided smile.

"I'm probably jumping way ahead of where I should," he started.

"Not necessarily. I've given you plenty of reasons why a new start somewhere other than Deer Creek might be a very good thing for me." The words seemed strange on her tongue, and rather freeing. Amanda's recent words rumbled around in her thoughts—"an independent businesswoman." She wielded the power to buy and sell, or for that matter to relocate. Marc's love had been declared in the Face Time sessions before she'd gotten on an airplane. They'd talked about nearly everything, except a move that involved her. The whole idea had come out of left field. Even though the kennel business was flourishing, she was determined to preserve an open mind to hear what the man with the sexy dimple in his chin had to say. Maybe she was destined for a new adventure to outdo the one she'd chosen by selling the farm and opening the kennel after losing her husband, Michael, and their baby all in one horrific week, now over three years ago.

His face brightened. "Sure you want to hear my shocking idea?"

She nodded, keeping a smile firmly in place. The real truth was that moving away from Deer Creek wasn't currently an option she was willing to consider even though her previous statement had indicated otherwise. She was pretty sure she'd experienced enough change for one lifetime. However, as her Grandma Clark used to say, "There's nothing as constant as change."

"I'm all ears."

CHAPTER 4

Gracie opened an eye to peer at the digital clock on the nightstand. It had been a late night of talking with Marc—in fact, they had talked until the restaurant closed. Breakfast time had come and gone at Red Hen Ranch. Sunlight peeked through the crevices of the bamboo Roman shade. She groaned, throwing back the covers. Angry voices broke into the stillness of the morning. Pulling the shade slightly away from the window, she saw Alex and Justin, the purported treasure hunters, hustled away from their tile-roofed stucco lodging by two men in Drug Enforcement Administration jackets. There was no time to waste on an extended toilette. She threw on jeans, a tank top, and ran a brush through her hair. She popped a piece of gum into her mouth, while slipping into sandals. There was no time for personal hygiene either. She crept down the graveled path, keeping a circumspect distance from the men, while trying to stay within earshot.

"You can't take us in without probable cause," Alex argued. "Besides it's medicinal," he added frantically.

"We need to ask you a few questions about the murder of Manny Enriquez," the agent with the shaved head responded coolly.

"Murder? We don't know what you're talking about," Justin snorted. He ran a hand over his scruffy face. "We don't know anybody named Manny."

Gracie stopped mid stride. Murder? So it was verified.

"Let's have a little chat in the ranch office," the other agent with a DEA cap directed.

"Hey! We're not going anywhere," Alex protested without success.

Gracie watched the agents escort the men into the Santa Fe. It was no surprise that murder was the verdict. She shuddered, remembering the battered face and twisted limbs. A good push to an unsuspecting victim would cause a fall from the treacherous switchback. Other guests had gathered, watching the little scene. Several had broad smiles with an "I told you so" look on their faces. Amanda appeared from the path to the henhouse, carrying a bowl of large brown eggs. Amanda jerked her head toward the rear entrance of the house. Gracie hurried to join her.

"Did you hear that Manny's death has been ruled a homicide?" she asked.

"Just did," Amanda answered. "I've given the DEA run of my office for the morning. We're on the list for questioning. Somehow, drugs are involved with his death. At least that's what the agents indicated."

"Drugs?"

"I'm afraid so. I can't imagine Manny being part of something like that, but people do strange things for money."

They entered the spacious and bright kitchen, and Amanda set the eggs by the sink.

"You missed breakfast, but there are a few pastries left by the coffee."

"I'll take the coffee, but I don't think I have an appetite this morning." Gracie quickly poured rich-smelling coffee into a mug from the large insulated carafe.

"I had an early call from Gary," Amanda continued as she rinsed and sorted the eggs. "He had a couple of agents at his house, along with Marc. Apparently, a special task force, made up of local law enforcement and the feds, are working the case now. Cocaine was found on Manny, from what Gary said, and the autopsy showed that it wasn't a heart attack or a fall that killed him." Her eyes welled with tears. "You think you know someone."

Her cell phone buzzed, and Amanda excused herself, hurrying outside to the courtyard. Hank entered the foyer, slamming the door behind him.

He strode into the kitchen and filled a glass with ice water from the large crock next to the coffee.

"Hi," Gracie greeted him. "Did you enjoy dinner last night?" The man avoided eye contact and quickly downed the water.

"Gotta get back to trimming mesquites," he muttered and walked away before she could summon up an intelligent response.

Amanda returned from the private residence section, a frown creasing her face.

"Hank works here?" Gracie asked. She hadn't seen him on the property before.

"Hank's a landscaper I hired a couple of weeks ago to start removing a lot of the mesquites on the back acreage. They've been a mess since I bought the ranch."

"He seems a bit touchy."

Amanda grimaced. "He's not very happy about the DEA showing up to question everyone. It is sort of intimidating."

"I can understand that. I've spent more time with police investigators than I care to remember."

"Really?" Amanda's look of incredulity made Gracie smile.

"Really. Somehow I've found myself involved with a few murder investigations back home."

Amanda's eyebrows rose in surprise.

"Not that I had anything to do with the murders," Grace added hastily. "I seem to have the weirdest luck when it comes to crime. Maybe that's why I'm attracted to Marc." She grinned.

"I'm not sure I want to know any more," Amanda quipped, taking a seat across from her guest at the large pine trestle table.

"I'd rather not get into all of it," Gracie said. "Why do you think we're being questioned again?"

"Because Manny was murdered, I guess. The agents were not exactly forthcoming on that. Fortunately for them, quite a few of the people they want to talk are right here, which includes us."

"How convenient. They seem to be extremely interested in the treasure hunters."

"I'm not surprised," Amanda affirmed. "Those boys are trouble. If I'd known how much trouble, I would have put the no-vacancy sign out when they arrived. They're doing exploration in the creek area, looking for a cache of gold that supposedly belonged to the Coronado expedition. Coronado and his men came up through Mexico and through the Huachucas on their way to find the seven cities of gold."

"Gold?"

"Yup. The old story is that some ragtag survivors of a shipwreck made it back to Mexico City in 1530-something with wild tales of seven golden cities with jewelers on every corner. The Spanish government was always looking for new revenue and backed Coronado in 1540 to check out the story."

"Which didn't work out, I presume," Gracie said with a chuckle. "So these guys think the Spaniards hid gold along the way or stole it from someone?"

"I guess. There's been a story around for a long time that a cache of gold was discovered on Ft. Huachuca back in the 1940s. There are also lots of tales about outlaws stashing loot in caves or burying it in the mountains. We've got plenty of notorious outlaws like the Clantons, and maybe these two are cut from the same cloth. If you ask me, they're up to something."

"Like what?"

Amanda shrugged. "Maybe drugs. I *do* know they were somewhere near where the maintenance team was working. Saw their vehicle in the parking lot yesterday, and Gary mentioned that the ranger ran them off an old mine near the trail repair area. They don't have a permit from the park service yet."

"Hmmm," Gracie murmured, hearing the office door swing open.

The two young men stalked out, eyes blazing, hands thrust in their pockets. Both were mumbling what Gracie assumed to be colorful expletives as Alex slammed the entrance door once again for good measure. The agent with the shaved head appeared from the office, his face hard and unsmiling.

"Mrs. Littlefield, can you ask Mr. Ramage to come in?" he asked.

"Sure." Amanda scraped back her chair from the table.

Gracie decided she really ought to make herself more presentable for a morning interrogation. She exited through the courtyard, eager to slip back to her cozy little house. She caught a glimpse of Marc stepping out of his truck through delicate leaves of what she'd been told was a velvet mesquite as she passed near the parking area. He saw her and waved. She stopped, waiting for him to join her on the path.

"In a hurry?" he asked, smiling.

"Actually, yes. I need to pull myself together for a police interview."

"Right. I was coming out to let you know that the case has taken a turn for the worse and to be prepared."

"So, the man was really murdered?" she asked, resuming her walk.

"Very much so. You saw that the body was in bad shape, but he didn't die from a fall. He was strangled with his own lanyard sometime the night before."

"Strangled?"

This was a strange turn of events. The twisted leg and battered face pointed to a fall. The narrow cliffs above the pool of water had seemed to substantiate her logic at the time.

"Mr. Enriquez was definitely strangled. His windpipe was crushed. The medical examiner confirmed it in the autopsy."

"How did he get so beaten up then?"

"That's what we're looking at now. There's a team up on the mountain trying to find where he was killed."

"Amanda mentioned that they found cocaine on him."

Marc shot a sideways look at her. "That's right. How did she know?"

"From Gary, the trail leader guy, I think."

"Oh." He paused, his eyes narrowing.

"What about the foster son? Has he been found?"

"Not yet. Uh ... before you sneak any more questions in, let me say that this is a drug case near the Mexican border. There are some really bad guys involved with this ... so ..."

"So, don't get involved," Gracie finished. She stopped at the arched azure door of the earth-colored stucco casita, her hand resting on a wrought iron door handle.

"Exactly. I've probably already told you too much, but in the interest of good police relations, you have all the information that should satisfy your curiosity."

"I'm officially on vacation, but you, on the other hand, seemed to be rather busy with this case. If you and I are contemplating a future together, let's say I'm interested because you're interested. It seems to be consuming quite a bit of your time."

Marc closed his eyes and shook his head. "Understood. But this is not Deer Creek, and you are not a police officer."

Amanda's gray head popped through the soft fronds of a large mimosa tree that shaded the casita next to Gracie's.

"Have you seen Hank?" she asked the couple.

CHAPTER 5

Jim sat in the kennel office, staring at the computer monitor. A frown marred his rugged features, eyes glued to where Cheryl, the kennel assistant, was pointing.

"It's the whole payroll, Jim," she sputtered. "The direct deposits didn't transfer. Are you sure you followed Gracie's instruction sheet?"

"Yes, I did everything," he insisted. "I don't know why Gracie didn't show you how to do this before she took off."

"Because I was on vacation right before she left," Cheryl answered with exasperation.

Jim looked at the slender woman and sighed. "I know. I know. You can write checks for everyone, and I'll sign them. I'm not calling her today. She was acting pretty grouchy after the software problem yesterday."

"She *is* on vacation and we *should* be able to handle 10 days without her. Can I look at the instruction sheet?"

Jim handed the paper to her. Cheryl scanned the precise instructions, which were typical of the boss' attention to detail.

"What about the passwords? There are two that have to be entered."

"I entered what it said on the sheet. Exactly. I'm sure."

Cheryl took a deep breath and sat down in the molded plastic chair in front of the desk.

"Are you still logged in?"

Jim looked back at the screen, which now read, "Your session has timed out."

"Not now." A black Lab with tags jingling trotted into the office.

"Hey, Haley girl," Cheryl greeted the dog. "I'll bet you're missing your mom like we are."

The dog wedged herself between the desk and Cheryl's knees to make sure a great deal of petting ensued.

"Excuse me, Haley. I need to look at the screen." Cheryl gave the Lab a gentle push. "Why don't I try signing in again, and maybe we'll get lucky. If not, I'll write the checks."

"All right by me," Jim conceded, leaving the desk chair available.

Cheryl slid into the wheeled chair and began typing the log in information carefully. "Wait a minute," she gasped. "The cap lock is on. No wonder it wasn't taking the upload. It's all case sensitive when you put in the file information."

"How did I do that?" Jim grumbled. "I'm tellin' you that I'm not touching this computer again."

"It's easy to do. I'll have this taken care of in a minute."

Haley leaned into Jim's leg, her face looking expectantly at his for attention.

"Yeah, I know, girl. Only six more days," he told the dog, rubbing her ears. "You'll have to put up with me for a while longer."

"There. It's done," Cheryl said happily. "We're all getting paid."

"Excellent work. Thanks." He stepped quickly to the office doorway, checking the reception area for customers. Seeing none, he turned back to face Cheryl.

"What do you think of this trip?" he asked.

Cheryl raised her eyebrows quizzically at the black-haired man, whose physique and good looks had made her a little weak in the knees when she'd first started working for the kennel.

"I think it's great that Gracie was able to actually get a

vacation," she answered in wide-eyed innocence.

Jim huffed and laughed. "You know what I'm getting at. What do you think about her and Marc?"

"I hope they're figuring things out. But it's really none of my business," she answered diplomatically. "What do you think of this trip?"

"I think it's a mistake, myself."

"Really? Gracie was pretty excited about spending time with Marc. She may come back with a ring."

Jim began pacing and gazing at the floor.

"I don't think she could handle being married to a cop. She ..."

His cell phone began ringing. Jim glanced at the readout and chuckled. "Speak of the devil," he said, answering the call.

Cheryl suppressed a grin, watching Jim's face light up. This little vacation was proving to be quite an eye-opener for the Milky Way Kennel staff.

CHAPTER 6

Gracie drummed her fingers on the arms of the overstuffed chair, waiting her turn with the DEA agents, who were grilling Hank at the moment. Oddly, his short-lived disappearance had tweaked Amanda something fierce. An awkward scene between the two in the kitchen had forced Gracie to relocate immediately to the reading room. She picked up a trail map that lay on the bench next to her, hoping the interviews wouldn't last long. Marc had left to take Max to a vet appointment for a follow-up on the German shepherd's foot injury. He'd promised a jaunt to Ramsey Canyon Preserve after lunch, which would be a welcome distraction after so much sitting around.

She traced a finger over the map, finally locating the trail she and Amanda had started yesterday morning. After the switchback, it evened out and wound gently to the mountain peak. She noticed that another trail marked Trail #283 led to two abandoned mines. That would be interesting to check out. If there was lost treasure up there, why shouldn't she have a look? Maybe she could get Marc to explore the sites. If the old equipment were still around, it would at least make for some unique vacation photos rather than touristy ones of Tombstone gunfight reenactments.

The office door opened, and Hank made a hasty exit

without acknowledging Gracie's presence. By all appearances, Mr. Ramage's interview hadn't gone well. The man's change of demeanor since their last meeting at the restaurant was odd. His friendliness had evaporated with no explanation. A sandy-haired DEA agent stood in the doorway, watching Hank leave. He smiled and motioned her into the office.

"I'm not sure how I can help," she started.

"We're trying to get an idea of times and the whereabouts of the trail crew when the body was discovered," the agent said, sitting at the desk. "I'm Agent Miller, and this is Agent Galvez," he said with a nod toward his shiny-headed partner. "Have a seat, Mrs. Andersen. I don't think this will take long."

Gracie felt her heart start pounding with anxiety as she sank into the leather club chair. She knew absolutely nothing that would help the agents, but why did she suddenly feel like a suspect? Disagreeable memories of quality time spent with Investigator Hotchkiss, who was relentless in her interrogation tactics, must be the reason.

"We understand that you accompanied Mrs. Littlefield yesterday. Were you with her when the body was found?"

"That's right. We were on our way to meet the trail crew."

"Did you see anyone around the area at the time?"

"No. Amanda called for help, and the guys came down within a few minutes."

"Who was in the group?" Agent Galvez asked, placing a foot on a square black leather ottoman and leaning toward her.

The agent's body language made her distinctly uncomfortable, and she tried to shift discreetly away from the man. What was he trying to do? Make her nervous?

"Uh ... the crew leader, Gary. I don't know his last name. And Hank Ramage."

Gracie looked the agent in the eye, hoping he'd back off. When he didn't, she rose from the chair. Sitting on its cushy arm, she gained a little confidence from the greater height.

"Anyone else?"

"Well, first the Border Patrol agents arrived. I don't know their names. Then the two men showed up, and then the park ranger."

The agent eased back from his intimidating posture and stood.

Agent Miller smiled and scribbled on a yellow legal pad. "What time was this, Ms. Andersen?"

"I didn't look at my watch, but it must have been around 9:00. We got to the trailhead about 8:30, I think."

"Did you know the victim, Manny Enriquez?"

"No. I'm here on vacation. At least, that's what I'm trying to do."

"Are you a friend of Mrs. Littlefield?" Agent Galvez asked.

"Well, not really. I'm staying here, and she's been kind enough to show me around since my boyfriend, Deputy Marc Stevens, who's on your special task force, has been working more than expected." She hadn't planned to throw out the cop card, but Agent Galvez was getting her riled.

"That's right," Agent Miller chimed in with a soothing tone. "What about Mr. Ramage? Was he with Gary Regan, or did he arrive separately at the scene?"

Gracie swallowed hard, her throat dry. "He was with Gary. They arrived at the same time." She glanced at her watch, hoping the dynamic duo would wrap up the excruciating interview.

Agent Miller stopped writing and stood. "Thank you for your time, Ms. Andersen. Enjoy the rest of your stay."

"That's it?" The abrupt end took her by surprise.

"That's it." Agent Galvez managed an unenthusiastic smile and opened the office door for her.

Apparently, her lack of beneficial information had earned an early dismissal, which suited her fine. She found Amanda in the kitchen, working at her laptop.

"That was short and sweet," Amanda commented,

looking away from the screen.

"Very much so. I'm not disappointed in the least. Now maybe I can focus on my vacation."

"I hope so. Is Marc coming back?"

"As soon as Max is checked out by the vet. I hope it's not a serious injury. If it is, it could ruin his chances for the training in El Paso."

"Marc's really counting on that training." Amanda closed the laptop. "It's all he's talked about lately. He and Cal really hit it off right before Cal was sent to Afghanistan. I don't know if he's said anything, but we sort of took him under our wing until he found an apartment that would allow Max as an occupant."

"Marc's mentioned your hospitality for those first few weeks and how helpful you were."

"We know what it's like to be in a new place and not have connections. Cal and I have always tried to help the newbies." Amanda sighed, tapping a finger on the computer. "I guess I'd better see how much Hank was able to finish this morning."

"Speaking of Hank, is he a suspect in this murder?" Gracie felt compelled to ask.

Amanda raised her eyebrows, frowning. "I'm not sure. Did the agents ask about him?"

"Yes. They wanted to know if he arrived with Gary."

"They asked me the same thing."

Amanda rose from her seat. She plucked a large strawberry from a wooden bowl on the kitchen counter and downed it with one bite. "Hank has been on the trail crew for a couple of months, but he's always avoided working with Manny. Hank's a bit of a loner. They would speak to each other, but I've always had the feeling that they didn't hit it off."

"Really? Hank told me that Manny was a good friend yesterday."

Amanda shrugged. "Maybe I have the wrong impression. Anyway, Hank's sure not himself today. In fact, he took off to work on another job a few minutes ago. Asked me if we could delay the rest of the work for a week or two. It's not an emergency job, so I'll let him cool off."

The sound of a vehicle pulling into the parking area caught Gracie's attention.

"Marc's back," she announced. "I'm going to try to talk him into hiking up to an old mine off the Hamburg trail."

Amanda laughed. "That's a pretty good hike. Be sure to take enough water if you go."

Gracie nodded and went to greet Marc in the foyer.

"What's the verdict on Max?"

"He's out of commission for a couple of days. The worst news is that we were turned down for El Paso," Marc reported glumly.

"I'm sorry." She felt the complete inadequacy of her words.

"I know. I know. It's stupid, but it happened."

"So, are you available for some hiking, or aren't you in the mood?"

"I should go check on Max. He's supposed to be resting for a couple of days. This is really going to put a damper on our plans."

Gracie's heart sank. Of course, he needed to check on his injured dog. She should help him and forget about the hike. It wasn't the end of the world. And Marc's world had now changed in a big way. Not snagging the drug detection training with Max was a huge disappointment. It could also be a sign that his "opportunity" wasn't quite right. Maybe he'd begin rethinking the Arizona plan. She certainly was.

"It's fine. It's kind of hot to be hiking anyway. I'll go back with you and help with Max."

"So, how's the big guy? Is he okay?" Amanda asked, entering the foyer.

"Not really." Marc recounted Max's medical woes.

Amanda tut-tutted and shook her head in sympathy. "Poor Max. You can't leave him in that apartment on his own."

"I know. We're headed back to sit with him. He's supposed to be kept quiet—which will be a challenge."

"So, you and Gracie are going to sit and keep Max quiet until she goes home?"

"Well, at least ..." Marc stumbled over his answer.

"It's all right, Amanda. Dogs are my business, and Max is a special case. We'll be all right." Gracie hastily came to Marc's rescue.

"Don't be crazy. Bring him over here. I'll watch him while you two go have a good time. He can hang out in my quarters. Molly and Cochise will be glad to see him too."

"That's a lot to ask," Marc hesitated. "He really needs to rest so the pad has a chance to heal well."

"I can do that. I'll turn on *Animal Planet* to keep him entertained. Go pick him up. Since the DEA boys seem to have monopolized my office for the day, I'll be working from my living room."

"Sounds like a good idea to me." Gracie brightened. Exploring the mine area was once again an option.

CHAPTER 7

By the time they'd reached the halfway point, Gracie couldn't recall what had made her believe a hike up the side of a mountain to see holes in the ground might be romantic. She stopped to take another swig of lukewarm water, while Marc leaned against the trunk of tree.

"How much farther?" she asked, trying to sound enthusiastic as she shoved the water bottle into the holder on her backpack.

"Not far." Marc glanced at the map. "Another mile probably. You sure you're still game?"

"I'm now committed to the mission," she half-joked.

Resting with Max might have been the better choice. They'd left him comfortably ensconced on a dog bed, with Amanda hovering, bacon treats in hand.

"All right. If we're going to make it there today, we need to move out."

"What a slave driver! I'm ready when you are," she blustered good-naturedly.

Gathering the remains of her dissipating stamina, she followed Marc through the trees. The rocky trail gave way to smoother terrain, and the elevation leveled off. The trail widened, and they were able to walk side-by-side.

"Have you had time to think about my idea?" Marc broached.

Gracie nodded. "A little bit. It's an exciting proposition actually. To establish a breeding kennel for drug dogs isn't anything that I would have considered."

She smiled, recalling Marc's passionate pitch at the restaurant. It hadn't been quite as romantic as she'd anticipated, but it had captured her interest. But her churning emotions about making such a wild change and actually thinking about Jim's reaction if she sold her share of the kennel was eating at her stomach lining. Then there was her house. All the remodeling and landscaping that she'd done in the last couple of years would be someone else's. The house would be hard to sell because of its proximity to the kennel, and the tangle of problems only worsened—her family being at the top of the list. They'd be totally shocked and probably resistant to support such a drastic new direction.

"The property that's perfect isn't all that far from the Red Hen Ranch. We can check it out tomorrow, if you want. I contacted the realtor."

"That soon? Well, good. You've talked with the breeders in Belgium too?"

She hoped her expression was convincingly positive, because everything that was wrong with dropping her irreplaceable business partner in New York was a runaway slideshow presentation in her mind. She felt as if she was on a teeter-totter, one minute up in the air about the possibilities of the new venture and the next slamming to the ground when faced with reality.

"I did right before you got here. Two of the main suppliers for the Border Patrol were in the area. One of them is looking to retire from the business, and he has three males and six females for sale. They're all excellent foundation stock. The property has a couple of decent outbuildings. We could have horses and ..."

Agitated voices filtered through the trees.

Gracie stopped, listening intently. "Oh no, it's Frick and Frack."

Marc followed suit, frowning. "Who?" He cocked his

head to make out the conversation.

"Sorry. Amanda's names for them," she whispered. "It sounds like the guys who're looking for treasure. They're trying to produce a TV show about their adventures, I guess. The DEA was very interested in them this morning."

"With good reason. Let's take it slow and see if we can hear what they're up to," Marc whispered back.

Gracie shadowed Marc's steps, carefully avoiding any loose rocks that might betray their presence.

The voices grew louder. Gracie and Marc entered a shady grove of pines slightly off the trail. Thick beds of needles deadened their footsteps.

The men were clearly visible below them and their conversation remarkably distinct.

"I told you. I left it in this cave. Somebody must've taken it," Alex grumbled.

"Are you sure it was this one? We left stuff in about a half-dozen places. I think you're wrong," Justin argued.

"It was here. I'm not an idiot. Somebody stole it. What are we going to do when the crew gets here? We don't have time—"

"Shut up, Alex. We'll have to move stuff from another cache."

"We don't have the frickin' time I said," Alex growled.

Marc inched forward and motioned for Gracie to stay put under the pines. She pretended not to notice. They squatted near a red-barked manzanita bush, peering through the tangle of leaves down at the pair. The men seemed to be searching in a large outcropping of rock.

A noisy group of hikers announced their arrival behind them. Gracie swung around to see several couples outfitted with walking sticks and binoculars amble down the trail. The pair below looked around nervously, quickly disappearing into the piñon forest. Marc stood, shaking his head.

"That's too bad. They took off when those hikers showed up."

"That group made enough commotion to spook all the

wildlife within five miles," Gracie added, brushing pine needles from her palms.

"Well, those boys bear more watching. I'll let the team know."

They quickly found their way back to the trail, resuming with the last turn to the saddle of the mountain.

"I'd love to know what they're hiding up here. Since the victim ... Manny was found with cocaine on him, I'm wondering if these two are stashing drugs around."

Marc turned and shot her a warning look. "Like I said, the drug business is extremely dangerous. Please stay away from those two. Don't give them any reason to take off. If they're involved, we'll pick them up when we have our ducks in a row."

"Understood, sir," she joked weakly. "Have they found that other boy? You know, the foster kid."

"No. The boy we found may cooperate, but we think this Ricky Fuentes may have slipped across the border."

"Why would he go into Mexico, and furthermore, how?"

"It's not that hard to get across the border, going either way. Most likely he has family over there who'll take care of him."

Marc's answer momentarily silenced Gracie. The only border she'd ever crossed was on the Peace Bridge, going from Niagara Falls into Canada. That was all very official and organized. Apparently, the southern border was a different story, or maybe she wasn't fully informed on borders in general.

"Is there any way to find him, if he's skipped the country?"

"Not likely. It's easy enough to disappear when you want to."

"If he comes back though or didn't actually leave, there's a chance. Right?"

Marc grunted noncommittally and then pointed toward the lower branch of a tree right ahead of them.

"Look there," he whispered, stopping to steer Gracie's gaze.

A striking red-breasted bird, with green and white markings, sat peering at them from its safe perch.

"Ohhh ... what kind of bird is that?" She reached awkwardly into her pack for the bird guide she'd purchased at the Nature Conservancy's store near the trailhead. Her sudden movement put the bird to flight. "Shoot. I should have this in my hand, I guess."

"We may see him again. Pretty unusual-looking bird though. This is supposed to be a spectacular area for birdwatching."

Gracie finally wrested the little book from the bottom of her backpack and began thumbing through the pages. "Aha! Here it is. An elegant trogon. That's gotta be it," she exclaimed. "Wow!"

Marc laughed. "If I'd known you were such a bird lover, I'd have taken you up here immediately. If you live here, you'll see this kind of stuff all the time. Maybe even bobcats or bears too."

"I'm not exactly sure that carnivorous wildlife is something I want to be acquainted with."

"They're more afraid of us, you know," he teased, stepping out of the shady trail into a patch of sunlight.

"Well ... not convinced of that, but it would be exciting to see one from a distance. A safe distance."

"All entirely possible as a resident here."

Gracie removed her baseball cap and swatted at the flies that kept pestering her. She caught his dark blue gaze, which had melted her insides when she'd first met him.

Marc had been the first on the scene to investigate a robbery at the kennel. He'd also saved her life a couple of times. His confidence, straight-arrow ethics, and twisted sense of humor had won her heart. The Harrison Ford good looks were the icing on the cupcake. Steeling her emotions against the gushy feeling that threatened to overtake her, Gracie decided to plunge into the topics she'd shied away from the night before, while adhering to her open mind resolution.

"Jim and I have a very successful business. My family

is all in Deer Creek, for the most part. Those I care to see, that is. I know zero about breeding Belgian Malinois, especially for law enforcement. You've already admitted you don't have the experience either. I see a huge learning curve and a lot of money going out and not coming in for some time. It's an exciting idea, but I don't understand any of it. Why are you even considering such an expensive business? Arizona is beautiful, but I don't understand why you want to actually move here either. Your career is in New York."

Marc's face hardened, his eyebrows drawn together.

"I know it's a big change, and not without some risks. This business venture could be ours, a new start for both of us. Max and I can try to find private training somewhere. I can go on to be certified as a trainer. It's a hand-and-glove operation. A business that'll only grow. These dogs are in big demand, and we could—"

"Wait a minute, Marc. You keep saying 'we' and 'ours' in all of this. What does that mean? I haven't heard where 'we're' going. Are we business partners or ... what exactly?"

Their eyes locked. Marc's face twitched slightly. Gracie had no intention of letting the conversation end. They would hash everything out today. Marc had captured her heart, but good business sense had to reign over her emotions. What was wrong with having a successful kennel in Deer Creek? Why had this almost crazy notion of breeding drug dogs and now training them come out of the blue? Marc hadn't mentioned anything about marriage or even her opinion about his decision to stay in the West. She'd been blindsided by the entire scenario. It was reminiscent of his decision to take the temporary position in Arizona.

Was he deliberately hiding something from her? Why? She needed to know what was going on. Marc dropped his gaze, removed his straw cowboy hat, wiping sweat with the back of his forearm against his forehead.

Another group of hikers appeared, breaking the tension. They murmured "hellos," and Marc shifted his backpack as if to move out when the last hiker passed.

"I really need an answer, Marc," Gracie insisted, grabbing the strap on his pack..

CHAPTER 8

Marc twisted around and grabbed Gracie's hand.

"Come over here," he snapped.

His grip frightened her, and she suddenly wished she hadn't forced the issue. He pulled her into the trees away from the trail.

"What's going on?" she demanded, snatching her hand from his.

Marc took off his pack, resting it against the trunk of a pine. His face was unreadable, alternating between anger and something else Gracie couldn't quite put a finger on.

"What's going on is that I'm without a job in three weeks."

"What?!"

She was at a complete loss. What was he talking about? He was a Wyoming County deputy.

Marc closed his eyes and took a deep breath before he answered.

"I don't have a job to go back to. Two weeks before you came out, the sheriff contacted me to let me know my position was cut. Two other people lost their jobs too."

"How could they cut your position? They're undermanned now."

"Typical budget woes. They can't afford everybody. Somehow, I made the chop list."

"But you're one of the most experienced deputies they have. Your record is stellar. They need you."

"But I don't have a family to support, and probably more importantly, some of my views don't always align with the sheriff's."

Grace huffed in disgust. "Is it a political move?"

"Could be. I've had a few encounters with the current sheriff that weren't exactly friendly."

Gracie pulled off her backpack, setting it next to Marc's. A welcome breeze cooled her damp shirt.

She grinned. "So, what you're telling me is that you're a bit of a boil on the sheriff's butt?"

Marc nodded sheepishly. "I guess so. Apparently, my opinions aren't always welcome. I could be wrong. However, the other two who belong to this special club with me have been known to disagree with him too."

"What about the state police? Or some other law enforcement agency?"

Marc grimaced. "No openings. Believe me, I've tried, and others have tried. I'm too old for some positions, and there seems to be a lack of personnel budgets everywhere."

"Then you've gotta get some support from the union or whatever you guys belong to. Can't they help?"

"The wheels of bureaucracy barely roll forward when it comes to actually helping somebody. Plus, if the sheriff really doesn't want me there, what kind of work environment is it going to be? He's early into a second term. I don't need that anymore. I hate playing games."

"So, why didn't you tell me about this when it happened? And this other deal with dog breeding. I'm really confused."

Gracie's mind was trying to reconcile several rabbit trails into a logical destination without any success. Marc had no job, but was thinking about investing some serious money into a dog-breeding program. Maybe he was counting on her money.

Marc's face hardened again, and his eyes seemed fearful. "I thought that maybe it was time for a second career. I have some money set aside that would give the business a decent start. Max's Schutzhund training gave him some extra points for the El Paso program, and I figured we'd be a shoo-in. But that's not happening." He sighed. "Initially, I thought we could take those skills back to Wyoming County. The county could really benefit. Then the two breeders came along at the same time I was handed the pink slip. They were visiting the area, watching the dogs work at checkpoints and border crossings. I happened to strike up a conversation with them and ..." His voice trailed off.

He kicked at the dirt and began pacing between a pair of boulders. Gracie sighed, searching for the right response.

"That's when a new life and business in Arizona seemed like a good solution to unemployment then," she said quietly.

"It did. I know it's harebrained and a lot to ask you to get involved in."

"My tirade about a boring life and escaping the familial bonds in Deer Creek only encouraged your line of thinking though."

"To be honest—yes. I know you and Jim have a good thing going there, but if you want something new and more distance between you and your family, this would be it." Marc stopped pacing and looked at her.

Gracie chewed her bottom lip, still hesitating about the real question that plagued her. Her cousin Isabelle's fingernails-on-a-blackboard voice echoed in her head, "A lady never asks that sort of question." However, Isabelle was over 2,000 miles away in Deer Creek and had her own romantic issues brewing. Isabelle could go kick a brick anyway.

"That leads us back to where we stand. Are you offering me a business partnership or something else?"

The distance between them instantly dissolved. Gracie felt Marc's strong arms press her tightly to his chest.

"I want you to be my wife. I love you, Gracie Andersen," he said, his voice husky with emotion. "But without a job, it's not the right time yet to, well … Please wait a little longer. Can you trust me?"

She pulled away from him, staring him down. It was an important question. Maybe more important than the one she'd wanted to hear.

"Yes," Gracie answered with conviction. "I can. You'll find a job. And soon too. I have no doubts about that."

Gracie was confident the kiss that followed was of the caliber Buttercup and Westley experienced in *The Princess Bride*. It was perfect. She even felt a smidge like fainting.

CHAPTER 9

Gracie watched as Marc gingerly removed the protective boot from Max's injured foot. The hulking black-and-tan shepherd licked his master's hand as if pushing him away.

"Sorry, Max." Marc refastened the boot. "I know it's not fun. Hey, buddy, it's looking pretty good."

"No sign of infection," Gracie concurred, looking over Marc's shoulder.

Max followed the pair back to the sofa, limping only minimally before lying down, his long black muzzle touching Marc's pant leg.

Gracie passed an admiring gaze over Amanda's comfortable living quarters. The great room was full of cowboy memorabilia on the walls. Gene Autry and John Wayne movie posters were in the center of one wall with belt buckles, spurs, and an ivory-handled Colt .45 displayed in several shadow boxes. Terracotta-colored tile ran throughout the space, with a couple of brightly woven Navajo rugs in front of the sofa and chairs.

Amanda appeared from her small kitchen with water in tall glasses.

"Is the foot looking all right?" she asked, placing a tray with the drinks on a leather-topped rectangular coffee table.

"It is," Marc replied. "Thanks for watching him."

"Not a problem. Anything to help the cause of love," she

laughed.

Gracie reddened and flashed her a wry smile. Despite Marc's assurance that he wanted to marry her, she still had nothing to show for it. And he hadn't actually proposed. Uncertainty seemed to be the name of the game when it came to her relationship with Marc.

"We've made some headway," Gracie managed, looking at Marc, who'd turned his attention back to Max.

"I hope so." Amanda smiled, and took a sip from her glass. "On the subject of progress, what can you tell us about the investigation?"

"Not anything really, Amanda," Marc said. "It's an active investigation. Speaking of which, I should check in and see if there are any updates."

"Spoken like a cop. I have a little news, though. Gary stopped in while you were hiking. He's been checking on Stephanie, Manny's widow. She's adamant that Manny wasn't involved with drugs in any way, shape, or form. Stephanie wants his name cleared and pronto. The DEA has torn apart her house looking for evidence and hasn't found anything. Plus, they still can't find Ricky. They're tracking down any relatives he has in Douglas and Naco, but, so far, nobody's seen him. Or will admit to seeing him."

"Ricky is probably the key to the whole thing," he said. "Although his record isn't good, he doesn't have a history of violence. A drug paraphernalia charge, possession of marijuana, shoplifting ... that sort of thing. If he's addicted to cocaine or anything else, all bets are off. When you need a fix, anything can happen. If he and Manny got into a fight, it's entirely possible he killed him. Ricky's on the run for a reason, and that's a good one."

Amanda frowned. "I know. The kid worked for me several times cleaning out the barns when Manny and Stephanie first took him in. He did all right and seemed to want a fresh start. Manny was serious about helping him do that. Ricky had a good deal going with them, if he could play by the rules. Manny was pretty strict."

"I guess he couldn't, unfortunately." Gracie adjusted a

small pillow behind her back. "However, he's not the only one who could be up to no good. Your favorite guests were spotted on our hike. They were a little off the trail. Engaged in suspicious activity, I'd say." She looked to Marc for confirmation.

"That reminds me, I need to make a call," he announced. He stepped out into the courtyard, pulling his cell phone from the holster on his belt.

Amanda turned her gaze to Gracie as Marc shut the door behind him. "Well, did he pop the question?"

Gracie bent over and scratched behind Max's ears, mulling over her response. Her love life had clearly become of great interest to her hostess.

"Not in so many words," she began cautiously.

"What does that mean?"

"I'm not sure myself. I guess we're still working out a few things."

She had no intention of sharing Marc's employment dilemma or his old-fashioned insistence on being the breadwinner. The investigation seemed a much more palatable topic.

"Where do you think this Ricky might have gone?"

Amanda raised her eyebrows and then smiled, apparently accepting defeat on the topic of romance.

"If I had killed someone, I'd try to get into Mexico. If he has relatives or friends in Douglas or Naco, I'm sure they could slip him over the border. It's not that difficult in a border town."

"Have you talked to Stephanie yourself about Manny and Ricky?"

"No," Amanda replied thoughtfully. "Gary's been doing that."

A sharp knock at the door startled the women. Max barked and struggled to stand, while Gracie held him. Amanda opened the door. Before them stood Ranger Ortiz, who filled the doorway with his imposing physical presence.

"Sorry to barge in, Amanda, but I'm looking for your guests, Alex Kramer and Justin Gardner."

"Are they in trouble again?" Amanda asked.

"No. Nothing like that. I need to let them know about the permit they applied for."

"They actually applied for a permit? That's surprising. I'm not sure where they are. Alex and Justin have been hiking every day until late afternoon. They're leaving here on Saturday morning, which is none too soon. I've had enough of their extracurricular activities."

"Those boys seem to be looking for trouble, but the powers that be are going to let them take a camera crew up to the old mining area off the Crest Trail."

"Interesting," Amanda replied, hands on hips.

"It sure is. They need some instruction on what they can do and mostly what they can't do up there. Do you have a cell number for either of them? The office didn't send it to me."

"Sure. Have a seat. I'll get it for you."

Amanda opened the computer that lay on the dark granite kitchen counter. She supplied the phone numbers, which the ranger scribbled onto a small pad.

"Thanks, Amanda. I'll track 'em down."

"Marc and I did see them up around Ramsey Canyon this afternoon, if that helps," Gracie offered.

The ranger raised his dark eyebrows and frowned. "Did you talk with them?"

"No. Nothing like that. We saw them a little ways off the trail. Not sure what they were doing. They didn't see us, though."

The ranger narrowed his eyes and smiled. "Oh."

"Marc was actually calling somebody about them." She hesitated. "To let the police or DEA ... uh, they seemed to be ...." She wasn't quite sure how to explain the spying they'd done on the pair.

"Don't worry about it. I'll talk to Officer Stevens on the way out. Seems to be a little complicated."

"You might say that," Gracie said with relief. "I'm sure he can explain it." She stroked Max's head, trying to calm the restless dog. He whined and pushed his nose against

Gracie's forearm. "Hey, Max. Settle down."

"New dog, Amanda?" the ranger asked.

"No. That's Marc Stevens' dog. Max cut his foot searching for Ricky Fuentes."

"That's too bad. Nice-looking dog."

"Thanks. He should be fine in a few days."

"Good luck then. Any luck that Ricky Fuentes had is running out. It's dangerous on your own in the mountains."

"Do you think he's still up there?" Amanda asked. "I'm hearing that he probably took off for Mexico."

"Could be, but he left Manny's vehicle in Ash Canyon. That tells me he's probably still in the area somewhere." He glanced at his watch. "I need to get back, so if you see those *gringos*, please tell them to call me in case I don't get a hold of them," he instructed, handing Amanda a business card.

"Sure thing, Armando."

Max settled down on the bed after Amanda closed the door behind the departing ranger.

"Interesting that Armando thinks Ricky is still up there," Amanda mused. "It makes sense with Manny's truck left in the parking lot."

"Maybe Ricky called somebody to pick him up." Gracie took a glass of water from the tray.

"That's possible too. I really hope he didn't kill Manny. I don't want to believe he did. I don't believe for a minute that Manny had anything to do with drugs either. He could have taken them away from Ricky." Amanda sighed, rubbing her forehead. "Manny and Stephanie did so much for the kid in only a few months."

The door opened, and Marc reappeared, tapping at his phone's screen.

"Geez. Interesting," he mused.

"What? Did they find Ricky?" Amanda asked.

"Maybe. An anonymous caller reported seeing Ricky in Naco."

"Good. Maybe he'll turn himself in."

"Maybe. If Ricky's connected to the cartels, the sooner he turns himself in to law enforcement, the better his chances of survival. His family could get caught in the middle."

"He needs to be found, Marc. The kid isn't going to slip away from the cartel." Amanda bit her lip. "He's got a big bull's-eye on his back."

"Everybody's doing their best," he responded, brow furrowed as he read another message on his phone.

"And you need to go back to work," Gracie guessed.

Marc shrugged his shoulders, looking uncomfortable. "Honestly, yes. But with Max and ..."

"I'll take Max to the casita so Amanda can get some work done. Don't worry about me ... for the moment," she added, her eyes twinkling.

"If you're sure ..." Marc hesitated. "I'll be back before—"

"Go. We'll be waiting for you."

The look of relief on Marc's face was worth the sacrifice of the remainder of the afternoon. Besides, his mind wasn't on anything other than finding a murder suspect at the moment. That didn't bode well for any conversations about their personal situations. Why couldn't life be simple? Why couldn't her vacation be a vacation instead of a police investigation? Food for thought as she meandered down the pathway to the casita with Max.

CHAPTER 10

A plethora of law enforcement vehicles filled Dominguez Street in the small town of Naco. Border Patrol trucks were the most prominent. A group of agents were crowded around two women inside a wire-fenced yard. A brown pit bull snarled and barked, straining at the heavy chain that kept him from rushing the perceived intruders.

Marc kept an eye on the dog, positioned near the rear entrance of the rundown concrete block home.

A Cochise County deputy spoke rapidly in Spanish to the older Hispanic woman, who kept shaking her head. Marc wished his Spanish was better, but language had never been his forte. Most of the conversation was lost on him. The younger woman twirled a piece of dark hair between her fingers, trying to look unconcerned. Her tapping foot betrayed her nervousness.

The deputy's stern face turned to the younger woman, and he reverted to English. "And what about you, Chaz, did you see Ricky today?"

"No. Of course not. He's missing. That's what we heard. Why would he be here?"

"You know we had a call about him being at your house today. He was seen on the street too. If he's smart, he'll let us help him."

She threw her head back and laughed.

"I'm not stupid, and neither is Ricky. He's not here. Hasn't been." She turned and yelled at the dog, "Shut up, you crazy animal!"

Marc stepped forward. "That's a good-looking dog. Where'd you get him?

The young woman hesitated, eyeing him suspiciously. "I don't know. He'll take you down, so don't mess with him."

"Wouldn't think of it. I'm looking for a guard dog. He looks like just the kind I need."

The deputy scowled. "I have a couple of questions," he interrupted.

"I'm done talking to you," the woman snapped. She turned to Marc. "The dog belongs to my brother. He bought him from some guy around town."

"Does he have any to sell now?"

"How should I know?"

"If you could help me, I'd really like to see if I could buy one. Maybe your brother could call him, or I could see him." Marc looked appreciatively at the dog and back to the attractive young woman, mustering his friendliest expression.

"He's working on a car for a friend. He won't be back until late." She began twirling her hair again, looking down the street.

"Thanks. Maybe I can catch up with him sometime." Marc stepped away, still smiling. He gave the deputy a discreet nudge.

The deputy took the hint, following Marc to the street. The Border Patrol agents straggled back to their vehicles.

"Whaddaya think you're doing, Stevens?" the deputy growled.

"Sorry, Travis, but I'm playing a hunch. Let's take a walk down this way and see if we can find her brother."

"Ah ... he's trouble. Probably in Mexico, if I know Ernie Sanchez."

"Humor me. Maybe Ernie's working on a car for Ricky, or maybe Ricky's with him."

"All right. I'll go along for a couple of minutes. Can't

hurt, I guess."

They strode past three more dilapidated houses. The sound of a revving engine to the north caught their attention.

"Back here," Marc said, jogging ahead of the deputy.

Turning left down an alley, a mobile home came into view, with a dirt yard adorned with scraggly cactus and vehicles in various stages of dismemberment. A beat-up brown sedan with the hood up was parked in the driveway. A man bent over the engine, while another sat in the car.

Deputy Travis Gunderson, a strapping 6'3" of coiled muscle, strode over to the car and pinned the mechanic against the grill when he tried to run. The driver scrambled to exit the passenger side. Marc met him as the door opened, his sidearm drawn on a frightened Hank Ramage.

CHAPTER 11

"What's the problem, deputy?" Ernie Sanchez seemed unperturbed, as he was patted down. "What about my rights? I wasn't doing nothin'."

"Ernie, the list of problems I have with you would fill a few pages. Whose car is this?"

"A friend's. Hank and I are workin' on it for him."

"Is this true?" Marc asked Hank, whose Adam's apple bobbed wildly.

"Uh ... yeah. Why are you hassling us? We're trying to fix a friend's car."

"Let's see the registration and insurance on this little number," Travis ordered.

"I ain't got it. We gotta get it running before he can put it on the road."

"Have you seen Ricky Fuentes today?"

"No, sir, señor deputy. *Mi amigo pobre* is lost in the mountains somewhere. I thought you were supposed to find him. He's probably hurt. And here you are wasting time talking to me."

"Ricky was seen in Naco today. I think you know where he is. Help him out by telling us. He's in bad trouble otherwise."

"Like I told you, he's not around."

Ernie was expressionless until he looked at Hank. The

change wasn't lost on Marc, who motioned Hank away from the car.

"What gives, Hank? What are you doing with Ernie?" Marc asked.

Hank turned his back to Ernie and looked at Marc with pleading eyes.

"We're fixing the car for a friend. I haven't seen Ricky. I don't need any trouble, so I'd like to get back to work."

Something was going on, but Marc knew Hank was not about to tell him the truth. At least, not in front of Ernie.

Giving the messy yard a cursory look, Marc and Travis tacitly agreed the cause was lost for the moment and left after telling the men to call them if Ricky showed.

"I know he's around here somewhere," Travis muttered. "But it's too hot to go looking right now." He wiped his forehead with a white handkerchief. "I gotta get some water."

Marc agreed. The afternoon sun was blazing, but promising rain clouds were building over the Mule Mountains and Bisbee.

The Border Patrol agents were sitting in their vehicles when Marc and Travis returned. One rolled down a window.

"Are we done?"

"Yeah. Thanks for the assist. Keep an eye peeled for Ricky though."

The agent waved and pulled out, the others in tow.

"Now what?" Marc asked.

"Beats me. At least we talked to Ernie. My big question is what's this Ramage doing with him? Isn't he a landscaper?"

"He is. And he was on the scene when Enriquez's body was found."

"That's what I thought." The deputy reached into his SUV and grabbed a lukewarm bottle of water. "Want one?"

"No thanks. Has anybody run a background check on Ramage?"

"Probably, but I haven't seen it."

"Can you send it to me if you've got it?"

"Sure." Deputy Gunderson finished the water and tossed the bottle onto the driver's seat. "Well, unless you have any other bright ideas, it's back to the drawing board."

Marc had a pretty good idea that if he kept an eye on Ernie and Hank, the missing teen might appear sooner or later. He drove past the trailer before leaving town. The car still had the hood up, but the two men were nowhere in the yard. Calling it a day, he turned off Willson Road onto Highway 92 to pick up Max.

***

Gracie had finished walking the property's perimeter, debating whether to call Kelly, her best friend, her soon-to-be sister-in-law, and the kennel's vet in Deer Creek. Another point of view might clarify the chaos in her head over Marc's insistence on getting a job before he proposed. Was he stalling? Maybe she was expecting too much. He was having a personal crisis. Then the time difference came to mind. It was too late to call, which was probably just as well. Gracie took a deep breath, willing her anxiety to subside. Approaching her casita, she glimpsed Amanda headed her way.

"What's the hurry?"

"I was coming to ask if you'd be interested in helping Gary and me get the equipment off the trail in the morning. It was left up there yesterday in all of the excitement."

"Sure. Marc's working tomorrow—big surprise. So I'm free.".

CHAPTER 12

The ride to the trailhead wasn't more than 10 minutes from the ranch. The parking lot was empty.

"Gary must have been held up," Amanda bent to double tie her hiking boots.

"Should we wait for him?"

"No. He'll catch up. I hope the cops didn't confiscate the shovels and other stuff. That wouldn't make me very happy."

Gracie agreed. The climb back up the challenging trail would at least work off Lupita's generous breakfast, a chorizo and green chile omelet with warm homemade tortillas. It was right up there with breakfast back home at Midge's any day. The morning air was comfortable, and the pair wasted no time reaching the waterfalls area. Amanda stopped at the pool, waiting for Gracie to catch up. Gracie was glad for the break. Her lungs were burning, and she needed to rehydrate.

"Hard to believe anything bad happened here."

Gracie nodded and drank deeply from her water bottle. Amanda's cell phone rang, interrupting the ugly memory of their previous visit.

"Are you coming? ... Oh. Well, we're already at the pool ... All right. We'll bring back what we can." Amanda hung up.

"So we're on our own?" Gracie guessed.

"Yup. He's tied up helping Stephanie. Both of her sons will be here sometime today, but he doesn't want to leave her alone in case Ricky shows up for some reason."

"I'm sure that makes Stephanie feel better."

"I'm sure. But, between you and me, I'm wondering about Gary right now."

"Why?"

"Gary got divorced a year or so ago. He's been very friendly with Manny and Stephanie, especially Stephanie since that became final."

"You think he's interested in her?"

"It appears that way. Manny made a couple of comments the last time we were out working on another section of the trail. Stephanie was with us that day, and she spent most of the time working with Gary rather than her husband. Manny didn't like it. At one point, he asked if she was going to help him or be Gary's personal assistant."

"Ouch!"

"You've got that right. It was pretty uncomfortable for a minute or two. After that, she worked next to Manny the rest of the morning." Amanda squatted, stood, and twisted her torso, groaning as she stretched. "I hate old age. All right, let's shake a leg. It's not that far now."

They trekked the last portion of the switchback above the waterfalls and easily reached the washed-out section of trail.

"Gary said there were shovels, a pickax, and a masonry hammer in this area."

Gracie scanned the damaged track. "I don't see anything."

"Me neither." Amanda rubbed her lower back. "I'll bet the cops picked all of it up. Now we'll have to find out which agency took it and try to—"

The snap of a twig cut her off. The women swung their gaze to the thick undergrowth.

"It's probably deer," Amanda assured her.

"There are mountain lions up here, right?" Gracie had a

feeling that someone or something was watching them.

Amanda shrugged. "There are, but I wouldn't worry about that." She pointed to the west. "Let's take a look above the falls. That would have to be the area where Manny was killed and then tossed. I want to see how it could have happened."

"All right," Gracie agreed, against her better judgment.

There was no way she wanted to linger on a remote mountain looking for a murder scene. Experience had taught her that two-footed creatures were far more dangerous than four-footed ones, and she wasn't truly convinced deer were the only things lurking in the woods.

"We're not staying long, right?"

"I want a quick look around," Amanda said tersely.

A rock formation towered over the waterfalls and stream below. A large flat stone went to the edge of the gorge.

"I think the fight could've been right here, and then whoever it was pushed poor Manny over the edge."

"But why didn't Gary and Hank see him on the way up? He would've been in the water."

"Good point," Amanda conceded, walking further back into the woods, away from the precipice.

Gracie decided not to follow Amanda. She again peered down at the water. It splashed merrily, a peaceful and reassuring sound. Branches parted on the far side of the pool, and two fawns daintily stepped into view. A small doe wasn't far behind, watchful of the perimeter, while her spotted progeny drank. Amanda had been right after all. The deer family disappeared into the foliage after their stop at the water hole. Amanda reappeared, looking aggravated.

"Find anything?" Gracie asked.

"Nothing."

"What exactly are you looking for?"

"I don't know. Something that places Manny here, I guess. I was looking for footprints or maybe a piece of torn clothing. Just something."

"I'm sure whoever is investigating has been over this

area with a fine-tooth comb."

"You're right. I'd like to help get some justice for Manny, somehow."

"I've been warned early and often about staying out of law enforcement's way. You can only do so much."

Amanda exhaled. "I'm not trying to horn in on our boys in blue. But it's personal, you know?"

"I understand that. We're a bit over our heads with this case though. Marc says it's a dangerous one and to keep a healthy distance. And I'm good with that."

Amanda seemed to acquiesce with the nod of her head, although the look in her eyes told a different story.

Gracie crouched and directed her gaze below. "Did you notice the trail that's on the other side of the pool area? I think it might be a game trail. I saw some of those deer you were telling me about."

"Where?" Amanda craned her neck to see where Gracie was pointing. "Oh, right. I wonder where it starts. Come on, let's find out."

She was already scrambling down the rocks. Gracie had no choice but to follow. It took a bit of bushwhacking to find the trail, but after a few minutes, they located the narrow path.

"I've been hiking up here regularly for a couple of years and never knew about this." Amanda pointed at the track. "Look at the prints. It's a regular highway to the water."

Hoof prints were abundant in the muddy trail. There were also some rather large paw prints, which instantly gave Gracie the whim-whams. A good-sized bear had visited the pool recently.

Amanda dug around in her backpack, finally pulling out a trail map. Unfolding the worn paper, she studied it, tracing a line with her finger. "Well, I'll be."

"What?"

"We're pretty close to the Outlaws' Cave. I've always used the Allen Trail, which splits off the one we were hiking, to get there. From here though, it looks like a quick hike. There are a couple of sketchy stories that Johnny

Ringo of Tombstone fame hid up in the cave, with some other ne'er-do-wells, after robbing a stagecoach. Some say they left the loot hidden in the cave, planning to pick it up when things cooled down, but never did. Since we don't have to haul any tools back, are you interested in giving it a look?"

"Sounds intriguing. I'm in."

The path dissolved after about 10 minutes of hiking, leaving them in a small clearing.

"Now what?" Gracie asked.

"Uh ... we keep going west, and then we should run into the Allen Trail a little ways over that ridge."

Gracie nodded, grateful that the ridge didn't seem all that steep. Pictures of a real outlaw hideout would most certainly be a hot topic of conversation with folks back in Deer Creek. Maybe they'd stumble upon a gold coin or some other unique relic. Howie, her insurance agent, would go crazy. He was an Old West aficionado of gigantic proportions.

Amanda's pace slowed once they pushed through a grove of spicy-smelling junipers. A pair of scrub jays, in their bright blue plumage, settled in one, voicing objections at a human presence.

"The trail is up this slope. There's a small box canyon. You'll see the entrance."

"Good. I was beginning to wonder about your 'short hike,'" Gracie commented wryly.

"Don't worry. It's worth it."

The trail wound down into a small canyon, lush with wildflowers, tall grasses, and oaks. The sound of running water greeted them. Gracie studied the area for the source. A rocky wash appeared with plenty of water, gurgling its way to the bottom of the mountain.

"Here we are," announced Amanda, stopping in front of a pile of massive boulders.

"And where's this cave entrance?" Gracie shielded her eyes from the sun's glare.

"Right through here."

Gracie followed as Amanda clambered through a natural Stonehenge.

Several precariously stacked boulders effectively hid the arrowhead-shaped cave entrance.

"Watch your step," Amanda called, picking her way through the rock-strewn floor. "Do you have a flashlight with you?"

"No. Do you?"

"I've got one. Come on. We can go a little farther back."

"What about bats?"

Gracie was quite sure she didn't want to meet up with any flying rodents.

"I've never seen any here," Amanda switched on her small LED flashlight. "But there's always the first time." She chuckled and led the way.

The cave walls trickled with moisture and the drop in temperature was instantly refreshing. Soon, the rocky floor gave way to a sandier surface with less to trip over. The ceiling was high enough for the average man to walk under without stooping. Cracks in the rock offered more light from the ceiling and she could smell fresh air entering the chamber overhead.

"No wonder it's so damp in here." Gracie pointed to the shots of sunshine, exposing water that trickled down the walls.

"This is the only spot where there's a skylight. Look over here. Everyone says this is where the outlaws and possibly Apaches had their campfires."

A ring of stones, with fragments of charred wood, was positioned in a spacious alcove tucked back from the main chamber. Smoke stains on the walls attested to cooking fires. A few battered, rusty cans, which probably held beans at one time, were scattered near the stones.

"This cave isn't on any of the maps and is off the trail, so it's not bothered by hikers very often," Amanda explained.

"Let me get a picture of this." Gracie pulled her phone from the back pocket of her jeans.

With Amanda directing her flashlight on the area, she clicked several photos.

Something clattered from the entrance, startling them. Amanda extinguished her flashlight when they heard the faint echo of voices.

"Who's that?" whispered Gracie.

"I think it's Alex and Justin. Listen."

The voices grew louder. Amanda pulled Gracie back into the alcove.

"I want to know what those two are doing up here," Amanda whispered.

Gracie wished she were lounging in the courtyard at the B & B. Her hostess seemed to have a penchant for leading her straight into trouble.

"We can distribute everything today," a voice from the darkness echoed. Gracie recognized it as Justin's.

"There are too many cops watching us," Alex complained. "If we're caught—"

"It's now or never. We'll lose our chance to make some real money, unless we can have everything in place."

"It's not worth going to jail for."

"We're not getting caught, so shut your face and do your job," Justin ordered, adding additional crude epithets for emphasis.

The pair passed Gracie and Amanda, who huddled in the darkness. The voices faded, and the women could see the wavering light from a flashlight proceed into the rear of the cave.

"We need to leave," Gracie urged, moving from the alcove.

"No way," Amanda hissed. "You stay here. There's a place where I can hide and see what they've hidden in here. They'll never see me."

"But, you'll—"

Before Gracie could finish her sentence, Amanda had already slipped away. She eased herself back into the safety of the alcove, breathing a prayer that Amanda wouldn't be caught. More arguing ensued from the treasure hunters, along with a few grunts as though they were lifting something heavy. Sweat freely trickled down Gracie's back, and her heart felt about to burst from her ribcage. If they made it out of there alive, she could only hope she'd never have to tell Marc about this.

She pressed her back against the jagged rocks, wishing for the power of invisibility. That was when her nose began to itch. Gracie pinched her nose, stifling the sneeze that threatened, which started a tickle in her throat. She clamped a hand over her mouth, feeling she might explode at any second.

Alex and Justin moved past her, hurrying back to the entrance. The coughing fit erupted ... seconds after the men exited the cave.

Amanda suddenly appeared at Gracie's side, eyes wide and a bit breathless.

"They've got drugs and other stuff," she whispered hoarsely.

"What? We need to get out of here!"

"That's not all. Look what I found in my hiding spot."

Amanda opened her hand and shone her small flashlight on a neon green plastic whistle.

"This is Manny's."

CHAPTER 13

Marc sat in the unmarked Sierra Vista Police vehicle in the Fry's parking lot, watching Hank load two bags of groceries into his truck. So far Marc's hunch hadn't played out the way he'd hoped. Hank had accomplished the most mundane of tasks: getting cash from an ATM, filling his truck with gas, and now buying groceries.

Marc's cell phone rang, breaking the monotony of his surveillance.

"Hey, Stevens, this is Gunderson. I've got that background check on Ramage."

"Great. How'd it come back?"

"He's not lily-white. Lost a landscaping contract with the Park Service last year because he was selling off old equipment that was going to auction."

"What was the disposition?"

"He's still making restitution and doing community service on the trail maintenance team to avoid jail time. He lost his contractor's license too. Plus, our victim is the one who blew him in."

"Really? What's the connection?"

"He's ... he *was* the hydrologist for the park. Apparently, Enriquez caught Ramage loading his truck with park maintenance equipment late one night and wasn't having any of the story Ramage spun for him."

"Interesting. So, he's not chummy with Mr. Enriquez, which is contrary to what he said in his statement. Anything else?"

"Well, there are a few rumors he might be working with a group to redesign vehicles for trips over the border, which lines up with what we saw yesterday. I'm goin' over to talk to Ernie again. I might find some interesting extra compartments in that old car."

"Thanks, Gunderson."

Marc decided to tail Hank for a little while longer, easing the car into gear. The pickup turned left onto Highway 92, headed south toward the Coronado Memorial. He was three vehicles back from the pickup when his phone rang.

"Marc?"

"Gracie. What's up?"

"Uh ... well ... are you available to meet us in a cave off the Allen Trail?"

"Why are you in a cave off the Allen Trail, and who's 'we'?"

"Amanda and I were hiking and decided to explore this cave. We accidently saw Justin and Alex in there. Fortunately they didn't see us. But Amanda found Manny's whistle in the cave."

"His whistle?"

"She says he always wore a whistle when he was hiking. You know, because of bears or mountain lions ... to scare them off."

"Okay. And where are you right now?"

"Well, we're resting behind some bushes near the cave. What do you want us to do? They might come back. And we think they've got drugs."

Marc hit his forehead with the palm of his hand. Hadn't he told her to stay out of this investigation?

"Stay put, and I'll try to find you. I need to figure out where you are exactly. I'll call the ranger. He must know where this cave is."

"Let me ask Amanda."

Marc heard muffled voices, and then Gracie was back.

"He might, but she's not sure. He came from another park in Texas a few months ago."

"All right."

"But Amanda says the docents at the visitor center probably know about it."

"I'll call them. Stay out of sight and don't touch anything."

"Uh ... all right."

He sighed. They'd touched something ... the whistle, most likely. What was it doing in a cave? The forensic crew had looked everywhere for it. In the water, all around the pool area, and above the falls. How far was this cave from where they'd discovered the body? So much for tailing Mr. Ramage. He punched the accelerator to make his way through the light traffic.

The two docents at the Coronado Memorial Monument visitor center knew of the cave, but since it wasn't on the trail map, neither one had an exact location. Ranger Ortiz was taking some vacation time and didn't answer his cell. Marc had to find Gracie and Amanda and fast, but he needed to locate the two suspects as well. More resources were definitely needed. He made a quick call to his supervisor.

At least he could focus on finding Gracie. It never rains but it pours. As if on cue, thunder rumbled. Magnificent cumulonimbus clouds were building over the Huachucas.

Stuffing the map in his back pocket, Marc ran to the car, hoping he would beat the rain.

***

"It's going to rain," Amanda confirmed the obvious. "And I don't want to get struck by lightning."

"I second that motion. I think we should try to make it back to the parking lot. Those guys have to be long gone by now," Gracie said. "Who knows if Marc will find us, and my phone doesn't have a signal."

Amanda held her phone up, circling it overhead. "Mine neither. We'd better hoof it."

"How far is it?" Gracie asked, fearing the answer.

"Not sure. Probably about two miles."

"Excellent." Gracie took a deep breath.

A crack of thunder motivated the pair into action. Leaving their leafy hideaway, Amanda led the charge.

Their ambitious pace got them to a marker that told them the Allen Trail was a half mile ahead. The breeze was full of the smell of rain. As if on cue, raindrops spattered Gracie's face, and she lengthened her stride. Amanda had her head down, focused on the path. The trail widened, the surface more dirt than rocks, making the way easier.

"I hope we don't run into Frick and Frack." Gracie was now able to walk side-by-side with Amanda.

"They're probably back to their vehicle at this point ... although they had heavy packs."

"Did you see the drugs?"

"I think so. There was a brick of something. It was wrapped in plastic."

"Just the one?"

"That's all I saw. They had some other things that were pretty interesting too."

"Like what?"

"Jewelry and some small copper bowls. Maybe they found real artifacts or maybe not. Those boys may have quite a scheme they're working on."

Gracie whistled softly. She checked her phone for a signal. Marc would want to know this. No bars appeared. Voices up ahead made the women stop dead in their tracks..

CHAPTER 14

Marc jogged Allen's Trail, while trying to call Gracie again. Her phone went directly to voicemail.

"Ugh!"

If he'd had Max, the dog would've surely picked up Gracie's and Amanda's scents.

The storm was gathering strength; the wind had increased, and a light rain hit his face. The cave was supposed to be off the trail about a mile from the parking lot. He glanced at the ascent ahead, redoubling his efforts to keep the pace steady. Thunder growled, and he put his head down to begin the climb, hoping to avoid the inevitable lightning strikes. The trail gave way at the top to more trees and bushes, where a trail marker indicated he had to choose between the Allen and #317 trails. He kept to Allen, hoping his GPS phone app was accurate. He was almost at the one-mile mark, where he needed to find a wash and then locate a little-used trail (probably overgrown, according to the docents) that would lead him to the cave. The ambiguous directions made him uneasy, but with a crucial piece of evidence and the love of his life in a dangerous jam, he'd find that cave. He had no other options.

***

Gracie and Amanda crouched behind a pile of rocks a

few feet away from the trail, straining to hear the male voices.

"Help me pick this up," Justin demanded.

"Hang on. I've gotta get this pack off first."

Another bolt of lightning arced overhead, with an ear-splitting crack of thunder close behind.

Gracie closed her eyes, hoping that Marc was somewhere close by. It seemed like ages since she'd called him.

"There. That's it. Come on. Move it. The mine isn't much farther," Alex said.

Amanda inched forward, with Gracie next to her.

"They're going off the trail," Amanda whispered.

"I see that. Did he say something about a mine?"

"That's what I heard. I don't know of any mines in this area."

Amanda scrambled up the rocks, watching the men disappear into a manzanita thicket.

"Come on, Gracie. We need to keep moving."

"Right behind you," Gracie grunted, scraping her hand on the rock's rough surface as she pushed herself up.

Amanda was off at a brisk trot on the level trail. Gracie hastily gathered a small pile of stones to mark the spot the young men had detoured. The rain erupted in torrents. She hurried to catch up with Amanda.

As they began their descent, they caught sight of a bedraggled Marc slogging toward them.

"Marc!" Gracie called, relief washing over her.

She flung herself at him, grateful for the safety of his arms.

"No time for mush," Amanda growled. "Let's get outta here!"

***

They watched the downpour from Marc's vehicle, the nearby wash raging with branches and rocks carried by turbulent waters. Gracie couldn't believe the empty wash from the morning was now a muddy powerhouse.

"All right, ladies, tell me everything," Marc demanded.

Gracie, feeling a lack of any moxie, left the telling of their cave adventure to the redoubtable Amanda.

"You left the whistle in the cave, right?" Marc's face was like flint.

"Of course not," Amanda sputtered. "Gracie wanted me to, but ... What if those guys found it or someone else picked it up? I put it in my pack."

Marc groaned.

"I'm not an idiot. I took a picture with my phone before I picked it up, several in fact. Here."

Amanda shoved the phone into his hand. She unzipped her green canvas backpack and carefully extracted a red bandanna, twisted into a knot.

Marc studied the photos and then took the cloth-wrapped whistle.

"It's Manny's for sure. It has a bit of white tape that covers a crack," Amanda assured him. "And before you ask, I picked it up with the bandanna, not my hand."

"Still not good, Amanda."

"Well, now you have it, and once you catch up with the Bobbsey twins, you'll have your killers."

"He needs to know what we heard on the way back," Gracie prompted.

"You mean, there's more?" Marc kneaded his brow. "OK. Spill!"

Gracie gave him the barest of facts and nothing about their hiding place in the rocks. It had been a bit dicey getting in and out of there, and they'd been too close to the treasure hunters. Considering Marc's current state of mind, she felt sure that any details along those lines would send him into low earth orbit.

Marc grabbed his phone from the console. "All right. Let's hope a team is on the way up.".

CHAPTER 15

The cave was full of crime scene technicians, lights, the DEA agents, and a couple of Cochise County deputies. Marc watched one of the technicians spritz Luminal in the area where Amanda swore she'd found the whistle.

Unfortunately for Amanda, Agent Galvez was rigorously interrogating her about why she'd removed a crucial piece of evidence from its location. He'd known this would happen. Amanda now looked like a very good suspect and hence subject to all sorts of questions.

"I think I want my attorney," she bristled. "You're twisting my words to make me look guilty. Even if I'd left it there, you'd say I planted it. This is a no-win scenario for me. Like I said before, I was afraid someone would find it and take it before you got here. I picked it up with the bandanna, like they do on TV."

She stomped off, hands on hips, reminding Marc of a foul-tempered hen from Amanda's chicken yard.

Marc needed to stay out of this interview. He was too connected. Gracie stood gazing into the cave, a million miles away from the vacant look in her eyes.

"A penny for your thoughts." Marc placed a hand on her shoulder.

"You don't want to know any of my thoughts at the moment." She scowled, glancing over at Amanda, who'd found a seat on a damp boulder away from the activity.

"Understood. She made a big mistake by picking that whistle up. If she'd left it alone and taken the picture, we'd be fine."

"Or if I'd witnessed her picking it up," Gracie added.

"You don't want to be any more involved than you are already."

"I think I'm up to my eyeballs in involvement. How did this happen? Hiking seemed like such a relaxing activity. Helping repair a trail. A little community service while on vacation. Exploring a cave. But no! A body in the water and now stumbling onto the murder scene. Unbelievable!"

"I know. You deserve a do-over on your vacation."

"I guess. But let me ask you this. What was Manny doing here? Was he involved in a drug deal or trying to stop a drug deal between Ricky and those two guys?"

"Good questions ... ones we'll be looking into. Meanwhile, I still maintain that Ricky is the key to the murder. It could be a drug deal gone wrong, and Manny was somehow caught up in it. I don't want to speculate any further."

"Hey, we've found something," a technician called from the cave.

"I'll be back," Marc promised.

The tech led Marc and the DEA agents to the niche where Amanda had allegedly found the whistle.

"We discovered some blood here on the cave wall and on this rock," he said, showing them an evidence bag with a rosy quartz stone.

"Good," Agent Galvez grumbled. "It's something."

"The best part is these fibers we found snagged back here." He held up another evidence bag with green nylon threads.

"The lanyard that strangled the victim was green. Looks like it could be a match." Agent Miller took the bag and examining the ragged threads before handing it back.

"There's one more thing," the freckle-faced technician added, moving back into a mound of rocks that formed one of the niche's walls. "You can hear water running behind these stones. We moved a couple of them back to take a look, and there's an entrance down into what appears to be another passageway. We found the fibers behind the rocks. The body was probably shoved down into this tunnel and went into the water somewhere below."

The law enforcement team gawped in astonishment as the two technicians carefully uncovered the opening.

CHAPTER 16

"What are they doing now?" Amanda griped, watching law enforcement and CSI techs scurry to haul ropes into the cave.

"They must have found something important." She felt the vibration of her phone in her pocket. She had a signal again. Go figure. Jim had sent a text. She quickly opened the message. Just what she didn't need: another business crisis. Except it wasn't.

"Please call. I have a question about Haley."

"Oh, great. What did that dog do now?" she grumbled.

She pressed two on her speed dial.

"What's up with Haley?"

"Well, I'm not sure," Jim answered, "but I think she may have eaten about five pounds of cheese."

"What? How could she do that?"

"That's a really good question," Jim said slowly.

"I'd love to know the answer."

"I thought I'd be nice, and so I took her with me to pick up party supplies for your Mom. There's a big bridge party next week."

Gracie sighed. There was no way Theresa Clark would have a major card party without lots of cheese on the menu. She probably had all three of her avocado green fondue pots on the counter. Of course, cheese was Haley's weakness. She'd pass up a steak in favor of a slice of good sharp cheddar.

"You left her alone with cheese?"

"It was only for a couple of minutes, honest. Your Dad needed help carrying some stuff out of the garage for garbage day. I'm really sorry. Should I take her to the vet?"

"I don't know. Five pounds? Really? You probably should. She'll puke her guts out, but I'd say Kelly needs to take a look at her. In fact, I want to take a look at her. FaceTime me back."

The video connection wasn't the greatest, but Gracie gave her unusually subdued black Lab a long-distance visual exam. The dog was lying in her parents' living room, panting and licking her chops. The wincing smile on Haley's face meant only one thing.

"She's going to throw up," Gracie warned. "You might want to get her outside before the blessed event."

"That's what I told Jim," her mother said, sticking her head in front of Haley. "She's going to blow any second."

"Here," Jim handed the phone to Theresa Clark. "I'll take her."

"Are you having a good time?" Theresa asked her daughter.

Gracie pasted on a glowing smile. "The best. It's been so good to get away."

"It looks like you're outside. How's Marc?"

Her mother was making a noble effort to speak casually. The tone gave her away, however. Gracie was certain a slew of questions would soon follow.

"My connection is breaking up, Mom. What? Oh, darn."

She ended the call with a swipe of a finger. That was close. She looked up to see Marc motioning them to the cave.

Both Gracie's and Amanda's jaws dropped when the now-lit extra cavern was revealed.

"Were you aware of the hidden entrance, Mrs. Littlefield?" Agent Miller asked.

"Absolutely not!" Amanda bent to look down into the

sloping passage. "This is incredible!"

A string of lights lit the slope, and Gracie saw the small cave they were in was a cover for a much larger one.

CHAPTER 17

The sunset boasted a palette of outrageous pinks, oranges, and purples brushed across the sky in bold strokes. Gracie stood by the casita, enjoying the display. After the day's events, she needed time to think. Marc was back out looking for someone—he hadn't told her who. He had less than three weeks of employment left, and he was passionate about making the days count.

Almost all of the casitas were now vacant, except for Alex's and Justin's larger abode, Gracie's, and two others occupied by retired couples, who were traveling together. The air was heavy with the smell of wet earth—the high desert's monsoon fragrance.

Mistee Olin strolled down the winding path toward her, carrying what appeared to be an armload of rolled-up yoga mats.

"Need some help?" Gracie asked.

"Sure. Thanks." Mistee maneuvered a half-dozen multi-colored rolls into Gracie's arms. "The studio isn't far."

"Getting ready for tomorrow's class?"

"Trying to. Amanda let me open the classes to non-guests, and I'm hoping for a good turnout. Are you coming?"

"Uh ... Maybe."

"You should try it. Yoga is total wellness for the mind

and body."

"I'm sure," Gracie agreed, dubious of her ability to bend into any yoga positions she'd seen. The activity might be a train wreck for the inflexible. "I'm trying to keeping my schedule free, since I might be dog-sitting for a little while tomorrow. My boyfriend's dog was injured in that search for the missing boy, Ricky Fuentes."

"That's too bad. Nothing serious, is it?"

"No. A cut on his footpad. It's healing pretty well."

"Oh. Good." She stopped, shifting the mats under one arm and reaching into the pocket of her shorts to pull out a key. "You know, I'd hate to think Ricky killed his foster dad. But he's pretty messed up with drugs." Mistee shook her head and frowned. "I went to school with his mom. She got pregnant in high school with Ricky. She's in jail right now for drugs. Always in trouble."

She unlocked the hand-carved door to the airy studio. Although small, it had a spacious feel because of the high ceiling and light hardwood floors. Several tall candlesticks, made from gnarled branches, were placed around the room. The scent of patchouli lingered in the air. Gracie helped the willowy Mistee stack the mats near the bank of windows that allowed an unhindered view of the mountains.

"What about Ricky's dad?" Gracie asked.

"He took off when Ricky was little. Never had a chance, poor kid."

"That's a shame. I guess he did some work for the ranch, from what Amanda says."

Mistee stopped arranging the mats and straightened. "He did. Hank worked with him. He offered Ricky a summer job, but he never showed."

"That's really good of Hank to try and help him. I know he was pretty upset, as everyone was when we had to go through those DEA interviews."

Mistee's expression changed instantly from friendly to frigid, as though the room's temperature had dropped twenty degrees. Apparently, Gracie had brought up a touchy subject.

"What a nice setting for your classes," Gracie said brightly, hoping she hadn't ruined a potentially informative relationship.

"Superb," Mistee agreed. She swept her arms upward like a ballerina. "The feng shui is perfect. Cleanses your spirit and frees the mind. You really should have me give you a massage at least. You look so tense, and your aura is dark."

Gracie couldn't speak about any auras, but the bags under her eyes were probably screaming her need for sleep.

"I guess the vacation isn't going quite as I planned. Finding a body and all."

Mistee nodded, studying Gracie's face. "That's why you're out of balance. Death has been close to you." Her voice quavered dramatically.

"Well, I'm hoping there isn't any more contact this trip." Gracie grimaced, feeling uncomfortable under Mistee's gaze. "I'd better find my way to bed. It's been a long day."

"Namaste," Mistee murmured, her hands in the prayer pose. She assumed a yoga position, her arms outstretched over her head and legs entwined.

As Gracie strolled back to her casita, she felt grateful for the small solar lights that assisted in her vigilance for snake activity easier. The whole rattlesnake business made her jumpy, although she had yet to see one.

She was about to insert her key into the lock, when Molly, the border collie, appeared from the darkness, with Amanda close behind.

"Anything wrong, Amanda?"

"The DEA agents are right behind me. They have a search warrant for Alex's and Justin's casita."

"Really?"

"Really. They've flown the coop. Probably in Rio by now."

That seemed doubtful, but it would be interesting to see an actual search warrant executed. The bulky agents hustled past Gracie without a word.

The casita had not been vacated, as evidenced by the

small piles of clothes scattered throughout the two bedrooms. The bathrooms were stocked with all the usual personal products. Their empty suitcases lay in a heap with no evidence that the occupants intended to pack up.

"Looks like they're planning on coming back." Gracie peeped through the doorway, while Amanda stood near the bureau.

"Maybe. Or maybe it's supposed to look that way," Amanda said, picking up a yellowed and dog-eared map from the dresser. She let out a low whistle.

"Don't touch anything, ma'am," ordered Agent Miller.

Amanda blanched. "Right. No problem. This may be a big help to you, boys. Look at this."

CHAPTER 18

The traffic on Highway 92 sped by Marc's unmarked vehicle, which was half-hidden from motorists. He'd parked on King's Ranch Road, glad of a small dip that camouflaged his presence. Be-on-the-lookout notifications (BOLOs) had been issued for Alex Kramer and Justin Gardener. They had records in California that included DUIs and assault charges. Two fraud-related cases had been dismissed due to lack of evidence. It looked like the boys were back in business in Arizona. How they'd managed to interest a reality TV channel in a show was beyond him, but that was probably a front for what they were really up to.

He hoped Gracie understood the urgency of his job when he'd left her at the B & B. She hadn't looked happy, and the long afternoon of questions and the discovery of the second cave had taken a toll. The task force was returning early in the morning to explore the cave with more equipment.

He sighed, leaning his head back against the headrest. This case was putting a strain on everyone and everything, including, he sensed, any future relationship he might have with the one woman who made him believe that love was again possible. However, due to circumstances (aided and abetted, he had to admit, by a certain amount of blundering on his part), the romantic strategy he'd devised to make her truly his own had gone seriously awry. If only he could catch a break, any break, in this case, he might with a small amount luck, be able to steer his love life back on course.

A silver pickup sped past, catching Marc's attention. He recognized it immediately. Hank was on the move. He needed to play out his hunch. Something was happening tonight.

The truck kept to the speed limit, rounding the curve and heading north toward Hereford. The sun was behind the mountains, and the car ahead of Marc turned on its headlights. He allowed a vehicle to pass him, putting more distance between him and Hank. The truck slowed, a left turn signal blinking. Hank was headed up Ash Canyon Road. Marc went past the road, deciding how much slack to allow Hank. He couldn't screw this up. He pulled into the entrance of Wildhorse Estates and turned around. He tapped his fingers nervously against the steering wheel while several cars kept him from pulling back onto the highway. There were plenty of places for Hank to disappear before he caught up with him.

Ash Canyon Road was empty of traffic in the increasing darkness. No silver pickup. The dirt road went on for quite a distance. There was a limited number of side roads that Hank could have taken. No vehicle dust trails offered help; roads were muddy and puddles abundant.

Passing Muffin Lane, Marc swung the car around. Hank's quick disappearance might mean he took the first road off Ash Canyon, which was Twin Oaks, and that led to Our Lady of the Sierras Chapel. The road crossed a major wash and then wound up the mountain to the huge statue of the Virgin Mary and a Celtic cross that overlooked the San Pedro Valley. He'd visited the place once at Amanda's suggestion. The view was incredible, but the sense of peace at the chapel had been the main attraction on that visit.

Entering the parking area for the chapel, Marc easily spotted Hank's pickup. The gate was closed to the upper parking. Maybe Hank was going to pray. Probably a good idea for him, Marc reckoned. Even if Marc's gut feeling was wrong about Hank's involvement in the current case, he was most likely working to outfit cars with hidden compartments to transport drugs. That meant another opportunity to get into deep trouble with the law.

However, the sign indicated the chapel was closed. Hank was nowhere to be seen.

Marc parked the car on the far side of the area next to a retaining wall, well away from Hank's truck.

He scanned the steps for any sign of Hank. He began the ascent to the chapel, climbing the stone stairway. He flicked on a small flashlight. The air was cool tonight, a relief from the afternoon's humidity. He counted off the cast bronze plaques that numbered the Stations of the Cross, grabbing the railing at one point. The path was awfully steep. A scuffling sound drew his attention to the immense brown cross towering over the Virgin Mary. He turned off the flashlight, treading carefully.

***

Agents Galvez and Miller pored over the old map in Amanda's office, while Gracie and Amanda cooled their heels in the reading area of the main house.

"I saw the cave marked plain as day on that map," Amanda said. "Those boys knew about it, all right."

"Were they hauling valuables out of there, and Manny stumbled across them?" Gracie conjectured.

"Maybe he took Ricky hiking up to the cave, and they had a run-in with Dumb and Dumber. Ricky may have taken off. I'd be scared too if I'd seen a murder."

"They may not be as dumb as you think if they've located long lost artifacts that they can sell. And then if they're into drugs too." Gracie paused. "A lot of money is out there to be made."

Amanda snorted. "If that's what happened, why didn't Ricky go to the police? He took off with a friend and then leaves him hurt in a canyon. You can't ever tell with kids. They run from where they'd be safe."

The agents reappeared, grim looks on their faces.

"Mrs. Littlefield, would you mind if we used your office in the morning to re-interview everyone on the trail maintenance crew?" Agent Miller asked.

"Sure ... I guess that's fine. Why do we need more interviewing? Really, this is too much. We've told you everything we know."

"That might not be true, ma'am. As you recall, you were reluctant to tell us everything only this afternoon," Agent Miller replied with the slightest touch of sarcasm.

"Okay. Anything to help catch Manny's killer." Amanda crossed her arms, a defiant look on her face.

"Thank you." Agent Galvez refolded the worn paper.

"What about the map?" Amanda demanded.

"Consider it evidence, Mrs. Littlefield. Goodnight."

***

A low moan caught Marc's attention. It came from somewhere in the rocks around the huge cross. Hewn rock stairs wound everywhere, and a waterfall splashed on southern side.

"I gotcha. Come on. We have to make it back to the truck," a voice urged. More shuffling around was coming from behind the cross.

"I don't think I can ..." a young male voice gasped.

Two male forms moved slowly down the steps to the front of the cross. Marc rested his hand on the grip of his pistol. He backed into the shelter of the Virgin's statue, watching the pair descend to the main walkway. The security lights of the chapel afforded enough light to identify both men.

Hank Ramage and Ricky Fuentes.

CHAPTER 19

Marc took a step forward. "Need some help?"

Hank jerked Ricky back, causing the teen to yelp in pain.

"What?! Who?!"

"It's all right, Hank. Let me help you."

Ricky's hair was matted with what appeared to be blood. His arms were a mass of lacerations. The boy was barely conscious, moaning, as they half-dragged the slight teen down the steep walkway to the parking lot.

"How did you know I was up here?" Hank asked, panting with exertion.

"I saw your truck," Marc said simply. "He needs serious medical attention and an ambulance."

Marc opened the rear door of the sedan, and Hank eased Ricky onto the seat.

"You can't do that. Then everybody will know. We need to get outta here and fast. I can't leave my truck up here either. If it's seen—"

"He needs help. I'll call for an ambulance."

"Take him in your car. We're all dead if they find us."

"Who's 'they,' Hank?"

"They ... and that's all I'm saying. If they catch Ricky, he's dead and I'm dead too."

"All right, but you need to follow me back. I'll give you

protection. Ricky too. You can't walk away from this."

Hank nodded; perspiration and fear covered his face. "Canyon View Hospital?"

"Right. Make sure you follow me."

Ricky was slumped over. Marc gently laid him prone across the seat.

"Everything's going to be okay, Ricky," he reassured the teen, shutting the door.

Hank unlocked the truck with his key fob and opened the door. The crack of the rifle shot made Marc drop to the ground. He saw Hank stagger, clutching at the door handle. Another shot shattered Marc's windshield.

"Get down!" Marc yelled, crawling to reach for his radio in the front seat. "Stevens, Special Task Force, needs backup. Man down. Shots fired at Our Lady of the Sierras. Lower parking."

"Ten-four," the dispatcher's voice crackled.

Marc drew his gun, looking at the dark mountain above him. There was no way he'd see the shooter. They were sitting ducks. The silence up above was as worrisome as the shooting. Where was the shooter or shooters? He crawled to the front of the vehicle, his back against the retaining wall, invisible to anyone above. The sour taste of fear was in his mouth. He tried to make out Hank's location. A dark shape lay under the pickup. Marc couldn't tell if that was a good or bad sign. He strained to spot any movement that would at least tell him if Hank was alive. Below on Highway 92, the welcome sound of sirens greeted his ears.

Two ambulances eventually pulled out, transporting both Ricky and Hank. Marc leaned against his car and took a deep breath. Agent Galvez walked from Hank's pickup, lighting a cigarette.

"You were lucky, Stevens."

"Don't I know it. Not sure why they stopped."

"They got Hank, and that may have been the point."

"Maybe. Let's hope he makes it, and we can talk to him

and Ricky."

"The kid's in bad shape. Dehydrated, cut up pretty bad, and a nasty concussion. He's the one we really need to talk to."

"I can't believe he made it out of the mountains down this far."

"Well, he's probably got quite a story." Galvez ground out the butt on the asphalt. "We have our work cut out for tomorrow. We're interviewing everybody on that trail repair crew again at the B & B. Something's not quite right about the stories."

"What's not right? You can't want to interview Gracie again. She's not involved in the case. I'd hate to see the rest of her time here ruined."

"Hold on. Your girlfriend isn't on the radar, but Mrs. Littlefield's escapade in the cave, now Ramage for sure, and the Regan guy—something's not adding up with their stories. Plus this B & B is conveniently located for all sorts of traffic. We need to take a look around there."

Marc fumed over the last comment. Amanda was no drug runner. He didn't like any part of the focus on the B & B. But, as he knew all too well, everybody lies to the police. He hoped that Amanda was guilty only of being reckless with evidence, not an accessory to a crime.

"Please tread lightly," he managed, working to keep his personal feelings buried.

"Don't worry about it. Remember: Ricky's capture is need to know only. Nobody, not even the hospital, knows we have him and Ramage. Too dangerous."

Marc nodded, recalling Hank's words all too well. The man was hanging on by a thread. It would be a miracle if he survived.

They watched the crime scene team pack up their van. The adrenalin rush had taken a toll. He felt wrung out physically and emotionally. If interviews were in the morning, he wanted to be present and coherent.

Before he could ask, Agent Galvez said, "Let me take

you home, Stevens. You won't be driving your vehicle anywhere. And here's the tow truck finally."

A flatbed tow truck growled its way up the incline. Agent Galvez met the truck and handed Marc's keys to the driver.

"Ready?" he asked, looking at Marc.

"Yeah. It's been quite a night."

CHAPTER 20

Gracie sat in the shady courtyard, enjoying her second cup of coffee and watching the hummers dive-bomb each other. They were feisty little things, so much fun to watch. Her bird book purchase was a big help identifying the diverse birdlife. She'd already spotted three different varieties: a broadbill, Anna's, and magnificent. All were beautiful with shimmering greens, purples, and bright pinks. Marc had promised to join her this morning after the trail crew interviews. Fortunately, her presence wasn't required for any of it.

Amanda padded glumly from her living quarters, Cochise and Molly running ahead, anxious to be let out into the yard. Once the gate opened, they were off on their rounds. Gracie thought she saw telltale signs of red, puffy eyes on her hostess. It hadn't been a restful night apparently.

"Good morning." Gracie leaned back in her well-cushioned wrought iron chair.

"It's morning. That's all I know or care to," Amanda answered dryly.

"Sorry about the repeat interview."

"Well, I guess I shouldn't be surprised. Everyone is being questioned though, so at least it's fair. Gary and Hank should be here any time. Have you seen the cops?"

"No, but I think I'll steal another muffin from the kitchen. Want one?"

"No thanks. My nerves are shot after yesterday, which has my stomach in revolt."

The front door swung open, and Gary entered, followed by Marc, Ranger Ortiz, plus the inseparable DEA agents. Amanda bit her bottom lip and silently joined the group inside.

"Where's Hank?" Amanda asked.

Gary looked at the floor, and Agent Galvez took Amanda into the reading room. Marc joined Gracie in the courtyard, quickly settling in at her table.

"What's going on?"

"It's Hank," Marc said. "He died this morning."

"What? How? Why?"

"He was shot last night. It's under investigation."

"Shot? He's dead?"

Marc nodded. "Yeah. I thought he was going to be all right, but it didn't work out that way." He grasped her hand, his eyes pleading. "Gracie, please don't go with Amanda anywhere or do any more hiking in the mountains."

"Really? Do you think Amanda's in danger?"

"It's possible. We need to sort out all the connections today. Otherwise, someone else may … get hurt."

Her ill-timed holiday had officially become the vacation from hell. Maybe she should consider trying to find a flight home. She wished he'd divulge the whole story of what was really going on. Marc's communication style left a lot to be desired. She and Michael had talked about everything. They worked side-by-side in the barn, always together. This relationship with Marc was far different than her expectations. She pulled her hand away, giving him a weak smile.

"Thanks for the advice. I should call and check on the kennel."

"Sure. The interviews are starting, and I need to be in there."

Marc left her finishing the cold dregs from her cup. She'd call Jim. He'd have a logical, unemotional perspective, which would help clarify this murky relationship.

***

Once in Amanda's office, Agent Galvez said, "Sorry I had to break the news about Mr. Ramage."

"I know. I can't believe it." Amanda blew her nose into a soggy tissue.

"While Deputy Stevens and my partner question Mr. Regan, Ranger Ortiz and I have a few follow-up questions. Nothing serious."

Amanda nodded, wiping tears from her eyes.

"What do you know about Mr. Ramage?" the ranger began.

"He's a landscaper. Or *was* a landscaper. He and Mistee lived together. She's the yoga instructor here. He's had a little trouble in the past, but he had made restitution."

"Did you know the trouble was with the Park Service?" the ranger asked.

"Well, sort of. Yes. I did know. Actually Manny had mentioned to me that Hank was in trouble over a contract with the Park Service."

"Did you know that Mr. Ramage had been turned in by the victim?" Agent Galvez asked, pacing around the small office.

Amanda swallowed hard. "I did. Manny wanted Hank on the maintenance team to make sure he showed up to do community service, which was part of the agreement."

"How did the two of them get along on the team?" Agent Galvez asked, stopping and looking at Ranger Ortiz.

"All right. Most of the time. Hank wasn't happy to be under Manny's thumb. It stuck in his craw that he was being watched like a kid. Manny wasn't always the nicest guy. He was tough, but he was really dedicated to keeping the trails in good shape. He loved the area."

Amanda twisted the damp tissue in her hands.

"Do you think Mr. Ramage wanted to harm Mr.

Enriquez?" Agent Galvez asked, taking a seat next to Amanda. The ranger sat on the wood-and-leather loveseat, scrutinizing her facial expressions.

"How should I know? He never threatened Manny or got into a fight with him. I can't see Hank hurting anybody, but then again, who really knows a person? I wasn't a close friend with either of them—not really. Hank worked for me on different jobs. He took a real shine to Ricky when he was here though. Ricky liked Hank too."

"Ricky worked for you?" Ranger Ortiz asked.

"A couple of times. Manny wanted to keep Ricky busy when they first took him into their home. He'd been hanging out with the wrong crowd, and Manny wanted him to know what physical work was like. Work off some steam and stay out of trouble."

"Right. That was nice of you." Agent Galvez kept writing on his notepad. "Did Hank, er ... Mr. Ramage store tools or supplies here?'

"Sometimes, I guess. He would leave stuff in the maintenance shed next to the chicken coop."

"Would you mind if we took a look in your shed?"

***

Gracie sat on the edge of her bed in the casita, phone to her ear. "So, that's the story, Jim. I'm thinking that I should see if I can find a seat on a flight tomorrow."

"You really want to come home?"

"Pretty sure. It's been a terrible excuse for a vacation. A dead body, a cave with maybe some treasure or a drug cache, and now someone else from this trail crew is dead. It's not very peaceful or relaxing."

"And Marc really doesn't have a job?"

"No. He's unemployed in three weeks. That's between us for the moment. He's not himself—I don't think he is anyway."

"I see." Jim's voice remained impassive.

"In the meantime, I'm cooling my heels waiting for him to wrap up this case, and hoping no one else is killed. I don't like this drug cartel thing at all. It's way too dangerous, and I don't want to have to worry about him day and night."

"But that's what he does. Law enforcement is dangerous. Gracie, if you can't handle his job now, then you won't be able to handle it if you marry him."

"I know. I want to handle it. He loves his work. I love him. I really love him."

After a pause, Jim asked, "If you do, then maybe it's better to part ways, rather than be constantly miserable about his work."

"What? I want to be with Marc, as in married to him."

"I'm not hearing that. Chief, you need to figure out what's best for you. Love may not be able to conquer all in your case."

"I don't think—"

"Rethink, Chief. No romantic thinking, but daily life stuff. He goes to work with a gun to catch bad guys. You have to decide if you can deal with marriage to a cop or not. It's simple."

"Not really ... oh forget it," she croaked, her eyes filling with tears. "I'll talk to you later."

She'd asked for it. Jim always looked out for her best interests, and that meant some tough love. However, Jim's failure rate in relationships was rather high. He wasn't exactly a shining example of how to succeed in a committed relationship. Rather than stewing about the situation further, she'd check flights to explore her options.

CHAPTER 21

The shed yielded no results for the agents, and Ranger Ortiz had more pressing business at the office. Hank hadn't hidden anything illegal or of interest to law enforcement.

Relieved that her interrogation was over and her property didn't harbor drugs or stolen goods, Amanda hurried back to the main house. Gary was walking toward his Jeep, keys in hand, when she stopped him.

"How did it go?" she asked.

"It was fine," Gary answered, his voice a bit hoarse.

"What did they want to know?"

"Whether I was in the area the night before you found the body."

"You weren't, right?" She kicked at a stone that marred the smooth sandy surface of the path.

"Actually, Hank and I were up there checking out what tools we needed to pack in. It was stupid not to have told them in the beginning, but it looked bad once we knew Manny had been killed the night before, and Hank insisted we keep quiet about it. I think he was worried about his probation. They say Manny was most likely killed between seven and nine that night. Hank and I got to the trail about five. The hike in and back didn't take us long. Less than an hour." He rubbed his forehead. "I didn't see Manny's vehicle either time I was in the parking lot. If he was in the area, it was after we were there."

"Did you and Hank leave at the same time?"

"Well, no. Hank took off ahead of me. He was meeting Mistee somewhere. That didn't sit well with Agent Miller, but even if we'd left at the same time, Hank can't confirm it."

Amanda shook her head sadly. Cochise hobbled toward the pair, tail wagging.

"Hey, boy." She scratched behind his ears. "How's the hawk situation?"

The ridgeback sat and whined as if giving his report.

Gary laughed. "He's got a lot to tell you."

"He always does. The hawks haven't gotten one of those chickens this year. His record is perfect so far."

"Good for you, Cochise." Gary patted the dog's head.

"So, are you headed home?"

"No. I'm going to help the guys that are searching the cave for any evidence. Agent Galvez wanted someone who knew the cave well to assist."

"I didn't know about that secret entrance. Did you?"

"Yeah. It's tough fitting somebody as tall as me through that little slide area, but Manny and I managed to squeeze through the opening one Saturday."

"Nobody ever said anything to me about that little detail."

Gary shrugged. "Not much to see. Another wild cave. The stream that runs through it though is interesting. Quite deep, especially this time of year. Manny was really excited about to add the stream to his mapping project."

"Bats?"

"Some, but not a real roost for them. There's another entrance to that cave about 500 feet from where you went in."

"Really? Why wasn't I aware of that?" Amanda's voice ground with annoyance.

"Can't answer that. I guess it's never come up. But it's all a crime scene now. In fact, it may be a drug drop-off."

"Did the lawmen say anything about Alex and Justin?"

"Just asked if I saw them the night we were up there, scoping out the work. I saw their truck in the parking area, but nowhere on the trail."

"They could've been at the cave."

"Possibly. If they're involved in drugs, then more than possibly. I need to hustle." Gary looked at his watch.

"Stay safe," Amanda ordered. She turned to walk toward the Santa Fe's front entrance.

***

Marc sat in his truck, fiddling with his keyring, undecided about his next move. He'd promised Gracie more of his time today. Ricky had been admitted to the hospital in protective custody and under an alias. Only Galvez, Miller, and Marc knew who he really was. At least for the moment, Ricky's condition prohibited any questioning, but the hidden cave beckoned, and the exploration of it was already underway.

Justin and Alex were still missing. Their vehicle sat seemingly abandoned at the trailhead parking lot. The duo had either taken off, or they could be in trouble.

He had a strong feeling he was in deep doo-doo with Gracie. The look on her face had said as much when she'd left for her casita. Solving the case could mean a job though. In a few days, he was without an employer and the pressure was on. He still didn't have any job prospects, although law enforcement friends were giving him leads.

The rosy picture he'd painted for himself of proposing to Gracie and returning to New York with a fully trained drug dog to add muscle to the sheriff's department wasn't happening. He was an outsider to her kennel business. Jim was a capable business partner who really cared about Gracie. Marc couldn't see himself in the mix there. He'd been stupid suggesting that Gracie leave everything in Deer Creek to run a new business in Arizona. Milky Way was a solid enterprise, which the independent redhead had worked relentlessly to build from nothing. It wasn't fair to put the woman he loved in that position. His desperation and the opportunity to breed dogs, which had seemed

101

intriguing, had only created tension between them. He needed to rethink the entire job strategy. Realistically, his focus needed to be near Deer Creek, but opportunities were slim to none in law enforcement, especially there. Hiring freezes and budget cuts had thwarted every resume he'd sent out.

He jammed the keys into his pocket, next to the ring box he'd been carrying for three days, and went to find Gracie..

CHAPTER 22

The fish tacos from the food truck at the farmer's market disappeared quickly from Gracie's and Marc's paper plates. The fresh corn tortilla, crunchy cabbage, and perfectly fried tilapia—they were actual competition for Midge's famous fish fry back home. They sat at the picnic table in Sierra Vista's Veterans Park, watching a steady stream of people visit the vendors' row. This city was entirely different than Bisbee—a modern military town, with Fort Huachuca flanking the west side. However, the mountain views were first-rate everywhere she'd visited so far.

"I didn't know you could buy yak or emu meat until now," Gracie commented, wiping her chin with a small paper napkin.

"You never can tell what you'll find at the market," Marc chuckled. "I told you this was the place to live. It's totally—unique."

Gracie lowered her eyes. "I see that, but honestly, Marc, I don't think it's for me."

"Bad joke. I know, and it wasn't fair to bring it up. You and Jim have a good thing going, and I'm not asking you to mess it up. You've worked too hard."

The knot in her stomach loosened at that statement. She could stop wondering if she was merely being selfish to want to stay put in Deer Creek—maybe.

"You really mean that?"

"You have my word." He grabbed her hand and leaned over the table to kiss her cheek, since she was still chewing a mouthful of fish. "And I've been doing some thinking about my non-proposal as well. All I can say is that I'm an idiot. I haven't been unemployed since I was 18. This situation rattled me and ruined everything that I'd planned. I was going to sweep you off your feet, and instead I've dug a hole for myself."

"You don't have to ..."

"Wait a minute. I have to apologize and now ask humbly ... as in on my knees humbly if a second chance is even possible."

Gracie fleetingly considered once again if marriage after Michael would work. She was terrified of losing Marc if they married. He put his life on the line every day as a cop. Michael had lost his life in a farming accident. No guns had been involved in his death. But she sternly reminded herself of the one thing she had learned, especially in the last two years, and that was no one had guarantees on life and that fear stopped you from really living. Romantic feelings aside, she had formulated answers that would pass muster for Jim and herself.

"I accept your apology. Now what, Deputy Stevens?"

Marc's look of relief made her smile.

"Will you join me for dinner tonight and explore our options in a more conducive setting than this one?"

"This setting is fine, but dinner sounds wonderful. What time should I expect you?"

At least she hadn't booked a flight home tomorrow. Maybe it was providential that there had been no seats available.

"How about six?"

He picked up the soggy plates and napkins, tossing them in a trash barrel. Gracie eased herself from the ridged metal bench, brushing a stray bit of shredded cabbage from her shirt.

"I'll be ready, on one condition."

"What's that?" A look of worry creased Marc's handsome brow.

"That you improve your communication skills and let me be involved with your life—job and all."

"That's actually *two* things, but I get your drift. There are things I can't tell you when it's job-related. However, what I can tell you, you'll know. Habits of a single guy, I'm afraid."

"I can work with that. And I'll try not to overshare my family drama. Like stuff about Isabelle."

"Agreed. Are you sure Isabelle is really related to you?" His eyes twinkled with humor.

Marc's phone interrupted Gracie's response. She took a couple of polite steps away while he talked. It sounded serious. Maybe there was progress on the case. He tapped the phone screen to end the call.

"Sorry, but I have to go."

"You'll have to drop me off at the ranch first."

"Absolutely. Remember, we're on for dinner."

CHAPTER 23

Marc followed the CSI tech who'd met him in the parking lot into the cool darkness of the underground chamber. Plant-covered rocks had revealed a narrow opening, high enough for him to stand upright to enter the cave. After a sharp right turn, floodlights illuminated the depths. Agent Galvez greeted him, motioning him back where technicians were examining the pebble-strewn creek banks. The fast-moving water sounded like Niagara Falls, thanks to the layered echoes. The chamber was large, easily accommodating the crew of eight working the area.

"What did you find?" Marc asked, raising his voice to be heard over the water.

"A couple of things. We're pretty sure Enriquez was killed in the cave next door and pushed down the slope into this area." Galvez pointed to the incline that was being examined by technicians. "There's blood trace on several rocks coming down to this area, drag marks, and we found some more fibers as well."

"Did his body roll into the water, or did someone push him in?" Marc asked. He tried to imagine the amount of strength it would take to pull or push a dead weight into the water.

"Somebody had to put him in. We think it's too far for the body to have rolled just right and hit the water. It's more likely some of those larger rocks would have stopped him on the way down. The killer probably didn't figure he'd show up anywhere above ground. We think the stream winds around and joins the creek that feeds into the pool where Enriquez finally landed. It must've been a pretty bumpy ride. A lot of rocks and a lot of water moving really fast," Galvez added.

"It could be possible, but hard to verify," Marc observed, wondering about the course of the underground stream and where it would first make an appearance above ground.

"We need some way to test the theory. If we had a dummy or a flotation device, we could send it through to see if it'll end up in the pool." Galvez walked to a rocky alcove and sat down on a boulder.

"Wasn't Enriquez mapping underground streams? How about calling the Park Service office to find out?" Marc suggested as he watched the swift, dark water.

There was no doubt in his mind that a body would have been swept away in seconds of entering the churning water. The creek was at least eight feet wide and probably about as deep.

The agent snapped his fingers. "That's an idea. I'll send one of the guys down now."

"Maybe we'll catch a break if he mapped this stream. And I don't see Ricky Fuentes managing to push someone as big as Enriquez down here and then dumping him into the water."

"It's a stretch, but maybe with adrenalin ..."

"I'm not convinced. One or both of our missing treasure hunters might have handled it though," Marc pointed out.

"True. We're looking for them. Their vehicle's still down in the parking lot." Galvez rubbed the back of his neck, yawning.

"What if they got themselves into some trouble? I'd say let's activate search and rescue out here to see if we can find them. Amanda and Gracie saw them yesterday headed back toward the Allen Trail."

Marc was tired of the DEA's uninspired pace. Agent Galvez looked like he needed a shot of caffeine or some sleep. If Marc had been in charge of the investigation, he would've had somebody looking for them last night, especially after the shooting.

Galvez stood and stretched. "If you want to arrange it, that's fine by me. I think the techs are wrapping it up here anyway. I need to see if Donny's gotten anything out of Fuentes yet."

Marc had understood that Ricky Fuentes was off-limits, but apparently Agent Miller already had access. It would have been nice to have known that earlier.

Swallowing a couple of pointed and rude remarks, he said, "I'll call my contact and get started."

He was beat too, but it felt like he was close. If he could talk to Ricky tonight, maybe all the questions would be answered.

Marc took a deep breath of fresh air, glad for sunshine and clean oxygen as he stepped out of the musty cave. The glint of metal in the grass caught his eye. Stooping to check it out, he found a gold pinback on the ground. Pulling a tissue from his pocket, he carefully wrapped it up and tucked it in his shirt pocket. The technician who'd led him to the alternate entrance exited the cave, hauling his kit.

"Ken, come here a second," Marc called to him, taking the tissue-wrapped packet from his breast pocket.

"Did you find something?" the dark-haired young man asked.

"Not much, but bag it and tag it. It was right here." Marc pointed to the ground in front of him.

"Sure thing. Hey, this looks like the back for a ..." Ken started.

"For a collar pin?" Marc offered.

"Yeah."

Marc nodded and strode off through the trees, searching for a cell signal. Finally finding two bars of signal, he called the search-and-rescue coordinator.

***

Gracie strolled through Old Bisbee, savoring the eclectic mix of art galleries, antique shops, coffee roasters, jewelry, and some shops combining all of them together. She'd borrowed Amanda's VW beetle for a temporary escape from the ongoing drama at the B & B.

A clothing boutique, Gypsy Threads, caught her eye with the promise of a clearance sale. Maybe she would find something new for Tom and Kelly's upcoming wedding.

Her eyes needed a minute to adjust from the sunny outdoors to the boutique's softly lit interior. She was pleasantly surprised to find a wide selection of brightly colored, comfortable-looking blouses and tunics. Now if she could find something romantic and alluring.

"May I help you?"

The familiar voice caught her off guard.

"Mistee! Uh ... What are you doing here?"

"I co-own this shop," Mistee answered with irritation.

"Well ... I didn't mean ... it's well ... I thought ..."

"Are you all right?" Mistee's wrinkled brow turned to something that looked like concern.

"I am. But I'm surprised to find you working, especially after Hank ..."

The blank look on the young woman's face made Gracie's heart sink.

"What about Hank? Has something happened? He never came home last night, and he's not answering his phone."

"Oh perfect," Gracie groaned inwardly, wishing she had kept walking by the shop.

"No one's called you?" she asked timidly, her throat suddenly dry.

"No. Well ... the sheriff called my phone early this morning. I'm so sick of this business with the cops, I didn't answer. They only want to harass Hank." She stopped with a sharp intake of breath. "Something's happened to Hank, hasn't it?" The woman sank against the large old-fashioned wooden counter, sliding down the carved surface to her knees.

Gracie dropped to the floor, putting an arm around her thin shoulders.

"I'm so sorry, Mistee. I had no idea."

"What happened?" Mistee asked, snuffling, her face red and muddy with makeup.

"You really should hear it from law enforcement, not me. I know that Hank was shot last night and he ... he ..."

"And he's dead." Mistee's voice was matter-of-fact.

"Yes. I'm really sorry. Is there someone I can call or ..." she asked, helping Mistee to a standing position.

"No. I'm on my own. What happened? Was it because of Ricky? Oh, Hank, I told you not to get involved ..."

"Marc mentioned nothing about Ricky. Was Hank trying to help him?"

"He'd had a call from him. He was still in the mountains and needed help. Ricky's cell was about dead, which is probably what happened to Ricky too. Oh, I can't believe it," she cried, hugging herself and rocking.

Gracie wasn't quite sure how to proceed in this stunningly awkward moment. Who knew where Marc was, and she had no idea how to contact the DEA agents.

"Why don't I take you to the B & B? Amanda must have some way to contact the right people for you. You do need to talk to the police. They'll have all the information."

***

Mistee leaned her head against the car window most of the way to the ranch. She offered no further conversation. Gracie was glad for the 65-mile-an-hour speed limit, which she used liberally to get them to the turnoff to the B & B. Amanda was weeding the large cactus garden at the entrance. Cochise and Molly enjoyed a small bit of shade under a mesquite tree, lying with pink tongues lolling from their mouths, supervising her work.

Amanda rose stiffly, rubbing her lower back. "What are you doing back so soon?" she asked.

"It's a long story," Gracie said, her face grim. She stood by the car door and pointed to the passenger side of the VW.

"Mistee? Why is she with—?"

"She hadn't been told, and I went into her shop, which I

didn't know was hers."

"Oh, my gosh! Didn't the police get a hold of her?" Amanda threw down her gloves and trowel.

"She didn't answer the phone apparently, and they didn't try to find her."

"Unacceptable. The poor girl," Amanda commiserated.

She marched up to the car and jerked open the door. "Come on, Mistee. I'm so sorry about Hank. Let's get you inside," she clucked, like a mother hen. The Little Red Hen B & B was aptly named, Gracie mused.

Cochise and Molly limped and trotted behind them into the Santa Fe.

Amanda opened a small territorial-style cabinet and located a bottle of Johnny Walker. She poured a stiff shot and handed it to Mistee once they were seated in her living room.

"Thanks, Amanda." Mistee sipped the drink with a shudder.

"I can't believe the cops didn't track you down. This is too awful."

"I was hoping you had numbers for the DEA agents. I tried Marc on the way back and couldn't raise him," Gracie said.

"I don't. I have Armando's number, but he's not really all that involved. Oh, maybe he'd have their numbers. I'll call him," Amanda offered, reaching into her bra for her phone. She went into the kitchen to make the call.

"Ricky has to be part of this mess." Mistee began to tear up again.

"Are you sure he called Hank?" Gracie asked.

"I'm sure. Hank felt sorry for him and knew how tough Manny was to deal with. I mean, Manny wanted to help Ricky, but Hank knew personally how Manny ..." Her voice trailed off.

"So, Manny and Hank didn't get along?"

"Not really." Mistee sniffed. She dug a tissue out of her purse and blew her nose. "Manny ratted on Hank over some dumb junk equipment. He said Hank stole it, but Hank said it was going to be thrown out. He was only … Well, anyway, Hank got in trouble and was doing community service to fix the trails. The judge set it up so Manny could keep an eye on him, which wasn't right."

"That sounds pretty tense," Gracie agreed.

Now she understood Hank's "friend" statement when they'd found Manny's body. Their bad blood would have immediately made him the prime suspect. It was also interesting that Amanda and Gary had never mentioned it. The next question popped out before she thought twice.

"Why would Ricky call him and not Manny?"

Because he knew Manny was dead was her guess. The teenager could very well be a murderer. And it was also interesting that the police hadn't mentioned Ricky this morning. Amanda hadn't made any references to the teen either.

"Ricky wasn't happy living with Manny and his wife," Mistee continued. "He's going to be 18 in a couple of months and out of foster care. Hank tried to help him by giving him a job, but Manny didn't want Ricky working with Hank. He was a bad influence, Manny said."

Amanda rejoined them, frowning at the phone.

"I got a number, but Agent Galvez isn't answering either." Amanda stuffed the phone back into place. She wriggled and adjusted her bra strap. "I left a voicemail. We'll see if he calls back. Now, what's this about Ricky?"

CHAPTER 24

Max easily jumped from the truck, whining as Marc snapped on a leash.

"You sure he's up to this?" Craig Ames, the search-and-rescue coordinator, asked.

"Yeah. The cut healed quickly. He's got a protective boot for rough terrain, just in case." Marc reached into the truck's front seat.

Max reluctantly allowed the cushioned leather paw protector to be fastened. He sniffed at it, dancing sideways.

"He's going nuts at home. He needs to be working. We'll see how he does. I'm not going to push it."

"All right, but it could be tough going in some parts," Craig answered, checking a clipboard. He turned to address his team. "Okay, everyone, you've got your areas. We're searching from Trail 829 to the Rufous Loop and the Allen Trail fork up to Trail 89. There are some washes and ravines they might have gotten caught in."

He grabbed the leash of a rangy chocolate Lab. "Marc, why don't you and Max partner up with Gravy and me."

Marc nodded, following Craig and Gravy into the forest, while the rest of the team, six men and two women with their dogs, dispersed onto the web of trails.

Max showed no signs of limping and eagerly kept up with the Lab. Gravy was an old hand at search and rescue, sniffing and steadily working his way up the trail. Marc kept a firm hand on the shepherd's leash. He was taking a chance allowing the dog to be back in action so soon. Another injury could sideline Max again. He didn't want him to overdo it in the first 30 minutes. They could be searching for hours.

Craig's walkie-talkie crackled with updates from the three other teams. No sign of the missing treasure hunters so far. Marc was anxious to locate the fork where Gracie and Amanda had seen the two from their position in the bushes. Once they were well away from the parking lot, he was on the lookout for the pile of stones Gracie had placed as a marker, indicating the direction the missing men had gone.

"Here it is," he said, catching sight of the pile of three flat rocks with a round stone on stop under a squatty, misshapen juniper.

"All right, let's head this-a-way." Craig hung a quick left with Gravy.

Max continued without any sign of tenderness, sniffing the ground intently, pulling hard against Marc's strong grip.

"Max might have something," Marc called to Craig, who'd moved off the trail toward a wash. He gave the dog more slack, and the leash was instantly pulled taut as Max lunged forward.

The shepherd whined, focused on the scent, easily scaling a small cluster of rocks and plunging down into a small wash. Water flowed at a trickle, and Marc jogged behind his dog, splashing through the stream. Looking over his shoulder, he spotted Gravy and Craig following at a brisk clip.

"I think Gravy's picked up something too," Craig yelled.

The Lab dug his paws into the ground, leaping to clear a low barrier of scrub and sending stones scattering into the water.

The ground softened and became grassy with only a few trees and bushes. Max slammed on the brakes, yipping.

"Oh, great! Did you hurt yourself, boy?" Marc bent to examine the dog's paw.

Max shied away, working himself toward a gravelly slope.

"I guess not." Marc tried unsuccessfully to grab the leather leash. "What did you find?"

A bit of barbed wire with a small sign was barely visible in a clump of grass at the bottom of the slope. Along with a skull and crossbones, the sign warned "Danger! Abandoned mines are deadly. Don't get trapped. Stay alive." The flimsy wire enclosure had been cut, and the ends dangled in the tall grass.

"We've got an abandoned mine," Marc shouted to Craig, who was making his way down. "Somebody's been exploring, by the looks of it."

"Watch out for unmarked ones," Craig cautioned, joining Marc a few feet from the enclosure. "Where there's one, there may be more, and who knows how deep they are."

Marc nodded, snatching up the leash and giving Max the down command. Craig made a careful circuit around the hole, watchful for any other signs of excavation. Gravy lay next to Max, both dogs panting. Marc cautiously peered over the side. The hole was about six feet in diameter.

"Anybody down there?" Marc called.

Craig shone a flashlight into the darkness, revealing muddy walls and a few puddles on the earthen floor. There appeared to be a tunnel to the west.

"Look. There's some rope down there. Seems fairly new to me."

Marc agreed. The length of rope wasn't old or frayed, simply dirty.

"Is anybody down there? Search-and-rescue team. We're here to help!" Marc yelled, his hands cupped around his mouth.

The drop was about 10 to 12 feet, from his calculations. He squatted, hoping to hear a response.

"Do you think the dogs got it wrong?" Marc asked,

standing and brushing the dirt off his hands and onto his jeans.

"Not likely. We may have a recovery on our hands, rather than a rescue," Craig said solemnly.

"Maybe. Somebody's going to have to go down and check it out."

"We need some more help." Craig unclipped the radio from his belt.

***

An influx of guests kept Amanda busy with check-ins and tours, which put Gracie temporarily in charge of Mistee.

"Can I get you some coffee or tea?" Gracie asked.

"No. That's okay. I need to call Hank's family, but since the cops haven't called back, I'm still not sure what to tell them." Mistee picked at her nail polish.

She leaned back in the chair and closed her eyes. Tears trickled down her cheeks.

Gracie couldn't understand why neither the DEA nor the sheriff's office had returned a call. Ricky seemed to be central to everything going on, and Mistee was the first person who actually had information about him. They needed to talk to the woman.

"So, Ricky was into drugs for sure?"

"He was mixed up with them really young. His mother led the way into the drug world. Everybody smokes some weed, but if you're hooked on the hard stuff, it's a bad scene. He was probably born a crack baby."

"Do you know where Hank was going to look for Ricky?"

"Not sure. He was in the Huachucas though."

"Was it Ash Canyon where they originally looked for him?"

"No. I don't think so. I'm really not sure."

Mistee rose from the overstuffed chair, pacing to the kitchen and back. Her cell began ringing, and she hesitantly answered.

The conversation with the sheriff's office was brief, and Mistee teared up again, blowing her nose into the tissue offered by Gracie.

"It's all true." She hiccupped, wiping tears from her chin. "He was shot. They won't tell me where or why, but he was positively identified by a deputy last night. His body was taken to the medical examiner in Tucson and won't be released until the autopsy is done."

"I'm so sorry, Mistee," Gracie repeated, wishing she wasn't flying solo. Amanda's presence would be more than welcome.

"I'm going to make those calls now," Mistee announced, clutching her cellphone. "I'll use the yoga studio."

Amanda breezed in seconds after Mistee's departure. Gracie quickly updated her on the sheriff's call.

"It's about time. The least they could've done was go to her apartment or keep calling. Unbelievable! And here's another problem. I have people coming in tonight for Alex's and Justin's casita. What am I supposed to do with their stuff? They were scheduled to check out this morning."

"That's tricky."

"You bet your boots it is, but I had Ida pack their gear into the suitcases. I'm going down to haul them up here. Have you heard from Marc?"

"No. I'm beginning to wonder about our dinner date tonight."

She looked at her watch. He was supposed to pick her up at six, and it was after five, with no reply to her call from an hour ago.

"Want a hand with the suitcases?" she asked, trying to tamp down the doubts she could feel bubbling to the surface about Marc actually arriving on time.

"No. Go get yourself gussied up. I'll handle the luggage."

***

With harnesses and ropes securely in the hands of search-and-rescue team members, Marc and Craig were lowered into the pit. They began crawling on hands and knees into the tunnel. Marc led the way, his headlamp illuminating the narrow passage. It was wet and smelled musty and stale. After about 20 feet, the tunnel opened up into a chamber of rock piles, and they were able to stand.

"Anybody here?" Craig called out.

Marc's light hit an object. He stepped forward to examine it.

"This looks like part of an old Spanish helmet, a conquistador helmet." Marc carefully lifted the rusted flared rim and partial headpiece from the dirt.

"Criminey!" Craig reached out to take the helmet from Marc. "How in the world did this end up down here?"

"Look!" Marc scrambled over a rock pile. "There's pottery, a knife, and ... Hey, what is this place?"

Several broken, brightly colored clay jars were scattered toward the back of the chamber, and a dull-colored dagger was stuck in a timber support beam.

A scuffling sound caught the men's attention.

"Back this way." Craig pointed into the darkness.

Marc found that the tunnel continued past the larger chamber into a second one that didn't allow him to stand erect. Craig followed, shining his headlamp into the dark recesses of the cavity.

"Who's here? Can you hear me?" Craig hollered.

"Search and rescue. We're here to help you!" Marc added.

The scuffling sound began again.

"It's back here." Marc gingerly walked to the left to make sure he didn't bean himself on the low ceiling.

The headlamp's beam shone on a man's hiking boot. A rope was around the ankle.

"I found somebody," Marc called.

He turned the light to identify the foot's owner.

Justin's eyes squinted against the glare. He was gagged, and his arms were bound tightly behind his back.

"I found the other one," Craig said.

His somber tone immediately told Marc they were on both a rescue and a recovery mission.

***

Marc gratefully unsnapped the harness and joined the aboveground team and Max. The sunlight and fresh air were welcome.

He patted Max on the head. "You were right, big guy. They were down there."

The dog wagged his tail, barking excitedly.

"Easy, boy. Settle down. We've still got work to do."

It was a tedious business extricating Justin and the now-deceased Alex. The gaping knife wound in Alex's left shoulder was sure to be labeled the cause of death.

A team member grappled with the tottering Justin to secure him into the harness for the trip out of the pit. Reaching the top, Marc grabbed the man and eased him into a sitting position on the ground.

"How are you doing?" he asked, handing him a bottle of water.

"All right now. I was sure I'd die in the dark down there. I can't believe you found me."

"You can thank Max and Gravy for that."

Justin nodded, watching the two male dogs meander through the grass, sniffing and peeing.

"Who did this to you?"

Justin's eyes widened in fear, searching the faces of the search-and-rescue team.

CHAPTER 25

It was past six. Gracie chewed the inside of her cheek, trying to control the potential landslide of emotions.

No call from Marc. Things at the cave must have gotten complicated. But a call, a simple call, to say he would be late or couldn't make it would have at least made her less anxious. Any number of bad things could happen in a cave—landslide, cave-in, a bear even.

Such was the life of a police officer's wife. It might be her life, and she needed to get a handle on it—if he ever proposed. She'd even refined her "yes" through varying stages of what Jim would certainly tag as gooiness to what she was sure was a dignified "yes."

As time marched on though, her perfect outfit and makeup would continue to suffer. Her auburn hair was curling in rebellion despite the straightening wand work she'd attempted. The evening was humid with no rain to cool off the air, which made her feel like her makeup was running. She was pretty sure her deodorant had let her down too. However, the sundress she was wearing was fetching. That had been confirmed by the elderly birdwatcher in the next casita. "You look fetching" had been the white-haired lady's exact quote. She was pretty pleased about the dress. It was a botanical print with a scoop neckline and handkerchief hem. It would be a shame to waste all her sartorial efforts by not having a nice dinner somewhere. Maybe she'd borrow Amanda's car again or ask her if she'd like to go to dinner with her.

She made her way back down the pathway to the main house, hoping that Amanda didn't have plans. As she approached the parking lot, she noticed the ranger's truck parked near the handicapped space. What was going on now? Maybe there was news from Marc. Maybe Marc's phone was dead, or he couldn't get a signal and had sent the ranger to let her know what was happening. Well, probably not, but it would have been very gallant. She hurried inside and found Amanda talking with Ranger Ortiz.

"Sure. Take a look at their suitcases. We packed up everything today. I had guests taking over their casita tonight."

"Thanks, Amanda. I need to make sure nothing was overlooked in the last search. I have a feeling they were hiding something."

"Any word on what's happening at the cave?" Gracie asked.

The ranger looked over and smiled. "They were finished up there a long time ago."

"Really? I haven't been able to get a hold of Marc in hours. They're done?"

"That's right. Everybody's gone home." He tipped his hat and followed Amanda into the courtyard, down the walkway to her living quarters.

She stood contemplating the ranger's statement. Her extension of grace and understanding were for naught. She was officially stood up. Several words came to mind, none of which appropriate for a lady's utterance. Besides, she might cry, and that would really mess up her face. She stalked off, deciding that she'd watch Netflix on her iPad and call it a night. She needed some sort of nourishment and then remembered there was microwave popcorn in her casita along with a microwave. It would do.

Kicking off her "cute sandals"—also the exact words of

the little old birdwatcher—she flopped onto the bed, tapping the Netflix app on her iPad. Her cell rang just as *The X-Files* was loading.

Marc's voice came across loud, clear, and almost poignant with remorse. Almost.

"Gracie, I'm really sorry. My phone wasn't getting a signal in the cave or the mine."

"The mine? What mine?" she demanded coldly.

"The mine I was in as part of the search and rescue after the cave investigation. I ended up involved with a rescue. I know ... I know our date is screwed up because of this, but we're closing out this case right now."

"Really. What happened? What did you find out?" she asked, excitement and concern thawing her.

"Uh ... I can't—"

"Right. Of course, you can't. It's about those treasure hunters, isn't it? Because Ranger Ortiz is here. Amanda's letting him search their stuff."

"He is?"

"Yes. Is something wrong?"

"Are you in the casita?"

"Yes," she responded slowly. "I'm watching Netflix."

"Stay there. Don't go anywhere, and make sure your door is locked. Please promise me."

"Okay. I will. What's going on?"

The call had already ended. Goosebumps ran across her arms as she jumped up to throw the deadbolt.

Maybe Alex and Justin were coming back to the ranch, and the police were in pursuit. She should at least let Amanda and the park ranger know. However, she'd promised to stay in the casita. On the other hand, she didn't know for sure why Marc wanted her to stay put.

Raised voices caught her attention. Gracie peeked through the drapes in the front window. The dim solar lights on the pathways didn't clearly define the two people headed her way, but the voices were familiar. Amanda was arguing with the ranger about opening the casita recently vacated by Alex and Justin. There was a family now in residence, and Amanda made her disapproval known in no uncertain terms.

"You don't have a search warrant for the casita now. I can't let you in. There are other guests in there. I don't even know—"

"Mrs. Littlefield, it's extremely important that I check the casita one more time. Your cooperation is necessary, and it's in your best interest to comply."

"What do you mean 'it's in my best interest'?" Amanda demanded.

Gracie shut the drapes. A good question that.

She realized then why Marc had practically ordered her to remain in the casita. Frantically, she made a call to Marc, sitting on the floor, her back to the bed, out of sight of the door.

"Gracie? Are you all right?"

"For the moment. But Amanda might not be," she half-whispered.

"What's going on?"

"The ranger has Amanda at Alex and Justin's casita, but there are other people staying in it now. I'm not sure if they're—"

"We're almost to the ranch. Is he armed?"

"Uh ... I don't know. I saw him in the house, uh ... maybe."

Why hadn't she been more observant? Squeezing her eyes shut, Gracie tried to recall her recent encounter.

"Yes. Yes. He has a gun. I remember now. Oh, Marc, he's really upset. He might hurt Amanda."

"Do you know where they are now?"

"I'll check the peephole on the door."

"Are your blinds closed?"

"Yes. I'm being careful."

Pressing her eye against the peephole, she scanned the small area visible. There didn't appear to be anyone around.

"I don't see anybody. Maybe he's left. I can't tell."

"All right. We're in the parking lot. Stay where you are, and don't open the door for anyone but me."

"Okay. Be careful, Marc," she pleaded, ending the call.

She pulled the blinds slightly from the side of the window, trying to get a better view of any outside activity. Lights were on in Alex's and Justin's former casita. She hoped the family wasn't there. That would complicate things even more. Amanda appeared from the doorway, Ranger Ortiz behind her. His gun, now quite visible, was firmly planted into her back.

"Let's check the sheds, Mrs. Littlefield. It must be here somewhere, and I'm beginning to believe you know exactly where it is."

"I have no idea what you're talking about, Armando. You've lost your ever-lovin' mind."

"I'm thinking quite clearly. It's cocaine, Mrs. Littlefield. A brick of it, which is worth a lot of money. You mentioned to us that you saw Justin and Alex with it the day you went caving. They aren't in possession of it now. Maybe you and the deputy's girlfriend decided to help yourselves and blame the *gringos*. In fact, maybe we need to ask her about it."

"I don't have the filthy stuff. And neither does Gracie. Leave her out of it," Amanda quavered.

Gracie's legs felt like pudding. Where were Marc and the cavalry? The deadbolt wouldn't keep the likes of Ranger Ortiz from entering the casita. And it wouldn't take much for him to pull the trigger, by the looks of things.

Exhaling slowly, she let the drapery drop back into position. She was a sitting duck and on the way to being a possible dead duck. The only other way out was the bathroom window. Could she get through it? There wasn't much time.

An eyeball measurement indicated the window's promise as an escape hatch. Standing on the toilet, she slid the window open and punched the screen out. The pounding on her door compelled Gracie to jam herself through, praying no snakes or cacti greeted her on the other side.

Landing on her hands and knees in gravel, she sprang to her feet and ran toward the parking lot. A shot rang out behind her and she fell flat on the stones, praying that she or Amanda hadn't been hit.

"Gracie!" a voice hissed from a shadow.

"Marc?"

"I told you—!"

"He's after me too. I had to run."

"Get over here."

An arm stretched out in the gloom, grasping her hand and pulling her into the scanty shelter of a mimosa tree.

"Stay here and outta sight," Marc commanded.

Gracie nodded, biting her lower lip. "Be careful, please be careful," she whispered.

She crouched near the tree trunk and watched Marc and two other darkly clad men move stealthily toward the casitas. By their shapes, she identified Marc's companions as Agents Galvez and Miller.

Another gunshot shattered the air. Gracie gulped, feeling sick. Molly and Cochise were barking from somewhere in the Santa Fe. Grunts and the sounds of a struggle were close by. She inched forward from under the fronds of the mimosa, straining to see if Armando Ortiz was in custody.

"He's over there!" Amanda yelled.

Gracie had no idea where "there" was and clung to the tree trunk. The bulky silhouette and heavy footfall of the ranger passed her location. He was actually getting away! Had one of the guys been hit?

She stood away from the mimosa, anger replacing fear. This was not happening. If he'd hurt Marc, she didn't care what it took. Armando Ortiz was going down.

Looking around for a weapon of any kind, she snatched up a rock that filled her hand nicely. David had done in Goliath with a stone. There was no slingshot, but she had a pretty good arm. She could at least slow him down. Gracie skirted the edge of the large cactus garden near the Santa Fe's entrance that was lit with small spotlights. She hoped there was enough light to locate the escaping ranger. The running footsteps behind her inspired a faster pace. At least she had backup. A strong hand clamped onto her bicep, pulling her backwards.

"We've got this. Get down," Marc ordered, pushing her to the ground.

Plopping onto the gravel, she watched the DEA agents follow Marc.

Ortiz abruptly slowed and zigzagged back toward her and the cactus garden. The lights at the front of the B & B were bright, and coupled with the garden lights, exposed his egress easily. He looked like a cornered animal, his face twisted into a dangerous snarl.

"Stop, Ortiz," Marc shouted, taking aim with his Glock.

Agents Miller and Galvez flanked Marc, barring any escape. Two other officers stood in the parking lot, shotguns raised.

The ranger complied and turned, his sidearm pointed in Marc's direction.

Marc fired simultaneously with the DEA agents. Armando Ortiz spun around, flailing his arms, backpedaling to regain his balance. Stumbling over the rock border, he seemed to pirouette in slow motion—almost graceful. He then fell face down into a large, fuzzy, tentacled cactus. If she remembered correctly, Amanda had identified the rather spectacular species as a teddy cholla—a real prize. Gracie closed her eyes in anticipation of what was coming. The white thorned cactus unceremoniously collapsed under the weight of its occupant. It wasn't pretty.

The body of Ranger Ortiz lay right next to the B & B sign: "Welcome to Little Red Hen Ranch. Enjoy your stay."

***

Extricating the ranger's body from the wicked thorns of the cactus took some time. Gracie didn't envy the forensic crew or the EMTs, who were, no doubt, racking up significant overtime.

Amanda stood in the parking lot, directing guests to their casitas via an alternate walkway. The law enforcement entourage, with their flashing lights surrounding the cactus garden, blocked the easy access. Once all the chickens had come home to roost—Amanda's words—Gracie trudged after her to the residence.

"Do you drink whisky?" Amanda asked hoarsely.

"Not as a rule, but tonight I'll make an exception."

"Good. I hate to drink alone."

The exhausted hostess poured two shots and handed one to Gracie.

"That is something I'll never get over." Amanda knocked back the brown liquid. Her eyes squinted for a second, and she poured herself another hefty shot.

"It was gruesome," said Gracie. "I can't wait to hear the whole story. He thought you had cocaine? He was involved with drugs?"

"Agent Galvez filled me in on some details. They were really hoping to take Ortiz in alive. But ... c'est la vie." She knocked back the drink. "He was the cartel member they've been tracking for months. They weren't sure who it was, but lucky for them, a witness came forward and identified Ortiz as the guy this afternoon."

"Things moved pretty fast." Gracie took a seat on the sofa.

The sip of whisky burned her throat, bringing tears to her eyes. She was definitely a Diet Coke girl.

"I guess. After tonight's exploit, I expect a full report from the DEA. I imagine there's a lot to tell. Well, I'm going back out there. I need to know who to send the bill to for repairs to my cactus garden. Cruddy federal government. They *will* pay for it, or I'll know the reason why. Do you have any idea how much those things cost?"

Gracie chuckled darkly, watching Amanda make her exodus. Standing to leave herself, she caught her reflection in the glass of a tall china cabinet and groaned.

The "fetching outfit" was definitely kaput. She wouldn't be wearing it again, that was for sure. Between the shredded fabric and the dirt, the dress was history. Before she could turn the doorknob, Marc entered, making her take a couple of steps back.

"You surprised me," she said, laughing. "I didn't think I'd see you again tonight."

"The DEA has things well in hand at the moment, and I'm extra baggage. And speaking of hands," he continued with a rakish smile.

"Oh no. I'm a mess, Marc. Really ..."

"You are the most beautiful mess I've ever seen." Marc snatched her hand and dropped to one knee. "I can't wait anymore. The box in my pocket is danged uncomfortable, so here goes."

Gracie looked into Marc's eyes, feeling like a teenager. Definitely a bit gooey.

"Gracie, I love you with all my heart. And, even though none of my plans have gone right, including our dinner date." He paused, taking a deep breath. "Will you marry me?"

"Yes. Of course, I will. Yes."

Her rehearsal for a dignified "yes" was for naught.

"Whew! Great! I mean ..." Marc struggled to rise and pulled the ring box from his pocket. The ring slid easily onto her finger, and the next-most-perfect kiss commenced.

CHAPTER 26

Deer Creek, NY

Gracie hauled the wicker picnic basket from the back of the RAV4, trekking to the two picnic tables mashed together at the Lower Falls in Letchworth State Park. Haley, her cheese-loving black Lab, overjoyed at a park outing, trotted happily with her raggedy sock monkey in her mouth.

Her brother Tom and his fiancée Kelly were already putting plastic tablecloths over the wooden tables, pressing thumbtacks into the corners.

"Little sister, you're by yourself?" Tom asked, taking the basket from her.

"He'll be here. He'd better be here," Gracie said, laughing.

"It's so good to have you back home, safe and sound." Kelly wrapped her arms around Gracie for a hug.

"No kidding. I've decided vacations are way too stressful. Work is actually relaxing at the moment."

"Sorry I missed your arrival last week, I was at a conference at Cornell."

"Don't worry about that. I needed a couple of days of sleep to function again."

A pickup rolled into the parking lot in the space next to

Gracie's vehicle.

"And here he is now," she said, pointing.

Marc carried a grocery bag, and Max ran to greet Haley.

"Good man, Marc Stevens. You've avoided execution," Tom teased, shaking Marc's hand.

"We want the full story on the Wild West adventure you two were involved with." Kelly pulled out a Tupperware container of macaroni salad and setting it on red-checked tablecloth.

"I'll let Marc start on that." Gracie tore into a bag of chips and placed them next to a bowl of onion dip. "But wait for Jim. He's pulling in now."

Tom stirred the charcoal in the old park grill and plopped enough burgers down to feed an army. Jim strode across the grass, carrying a red cooler.

"Hey, Jim. Open that up. I need an adult beverage while Marc gives us the lowdown on Gracie's *National Lampoon* vacation.

Jim smiled and obliged. "I told her to stay home, but you know your sister. Never listens to anybody."

"All right, Peanut Gallery." Gracie grabbed a Diet Coke. "I would have to say that it didn't work out quite as planned, but the ending was pretty good. Right, Marc?"

"I would say so. Shall I or will you?" he asked. He pulled her close.

The trio looked at Gracie and then Marc.

"I believe I can guess," Kelly started.

"I'm sure you can, but it's official," Gracie confirmed. She twisted the diamond ring into the correct position for all to see. "We're engaged."

Kelly squealed, grabbing Gracie and hugging her. "Let me see that ring!"

"Congratulations! It's about time," Tom said, pumping Marc's hand. "Welcome to the asylum. You'll get used to it."

Marc laughed. "I am. I am. It's really not that bad," he grinned. He bent down and kissed Gracie soundly on the mouth.

"Congratulations, you two." Jim's look of uncertainty

gave Gracie a cold chill in the warm night. She should have told him before everyone else, but it was too late now.

The smell of burning meat returned Tom's attention to the grill. Jim grabbed a beer from the ice chest, popping the top.

"Have you set a date?" Kelly asked, sliding onto the bench seat, still looking at the pear-shaped diamond.

"Let's talk about that later," Gracie said. "Personally I want to hear the conclusion of Marc's last case as an Arizona lawman. I haven't heard the final outcome on the whole thing."

"Right. Come on, Marc," Kelly chided. "Gracie promised you'd have more details since it was closed now."

Marc straddled the bench seat across from Gracie. "Yes, that's right. The Park Service ranger was actually a cartel member who was using teenagers in the Sierra Vista area as his mules. Manny Enriquez, the Park Service hydrologist, must have seen him with his foster kid up on a trail. According to Ricky, Manny followed Ricky and his friend to a cave that was being used as a drop-off for cocaine and other drugs."

"That's the cave with the secret entrance I told you about," Gracie added.

Kelly shook her head. "Only you would discover a cave with a secret entrance." Please continue, Marc."

"Well, Ortiz, the ranger was there, and Manny confronted him. The two men fought, while Ricky and his friend took off. Ortiz ended up strangling Manny with his own lanyard and dumped his body into the stream that was in the cave. That stream runs underground and feeds into another stream which empties into the pool where Gracie found the body."

"It's amazing that the body ever showed up." Tom shoveled burgers onto a paper plate and placing it on the table.

"Funny thing is," Marc went on, "this Manny was working on mapping the underground streams for a study he was doing. His maps actually helped us verify that the murder scene was correct, and it was totally possible for the body to end up in Miner's Springs."

Jim, who'd been standing at a distance, took a seat next to Marc.

"What about those two treasure hunters?" he asked.

"Unfortunately, one of them was killed by Ortiz."

Gracie jumped in. "The ranger thought they'd taken a brick of cocaine from the cave, since that's what Amanda, the B & B owner, had reported to the investigators. That landed us in big trouble," she added, closing her eyes.

"The brick she saw was actually a box of trinkets the two were using to salt caves and abandoned mines. They had pottery, a Spanish helmet, jewelry, and all kinds of other stuff they'd bought from a replica place. Their big mistake was stashing a load of it in Ortiz's drop," Marc finished.

"Why were they doing that?" Jim asked.

"For a TV show," Gracie answered. "They were trying to wrangle financing for a reality series."

"What happened to the one who survived?" Tom asked.

"Justin's working out a deal with the feds for some fraud charges and not having the permits he needed. I doubt if he'll get more than slap on the wrist. He's paid heavily for a get-rich-quick scheme, and Alex lost his life over it," Marc said.

"Pretty grim outcome." Tom waved everyone to the food table.

"And Ricky," Gracie probed. "Is he safe?"

Marc nodded. "He is. It's terrible that Hank lost his life to rescue the kid the night I followed him to Our Lady of the Sierras. I wish I'd done more."

"You were in as much danger." Gracie frowned. "You could've been shot that night too."

"But I wasn't," Marc said firmly, meeting Gracie's eyes. "Fortunately, Ortiz only got the windshield. Ricky was the key to the case. He'd been dealing drugs for over a year when the ranger was transferred from Great Bend National Park in Texas and became the new cartel sales rep in the area. I'm crossing my fingers Ricky stays clean and decides to move on to a better life."

"I really feel sorry for Amanda." Gracie squirted ketchup on a rather crusty blackened burger. Her brother wasn't known for his grilling prowess. "She was sure the box was a brick of drugs, which led to Alex and Justin getting into real trouble."

"I'm not sure I'd recognize a brick of cocaine. How would she?" Jim asked, taking a bite of burger.

"TV, I guess," Gracie answered. "The cave was pretty dark, and it was a mistake easy enough to make."

"Ortiz was out on the trails, scouting for Ricky, and heard about Amanda's report from the DEA agents," Marc continued. "It was pretty easy to trap them in the old mine. When Alex put up a fight, Ortiz grabbed the fake relic knife they had and stabbed him. Justin was tied up and left to cool his heels. Ortiz was hoping he'd cough up the location of the drugs after he'd sat in the dark for a day or two."

"So, there were drugs missing then?" Tom asked.

"We believe Manny had broken into a package, which is why he had traces of cocaine under his fingernails. Ricky may have grabbed it and run in the confusion, or maybe it landed in the water. We're not sure exactly what happened, but Ortiz would have been extremely interested in recovering that valuable white brick."

"A tale of the modern Wild West," Tom commented. "So, are you back to work at the sheriff's department?"

"That's another story," Marc said hesitantly. "I actually got the ax a few weeks ago. The official version is budget problems."

"Marc has an interview this week though," Gracie added hastily.

"Right. It's for corporate security. The company is in Batavia." Marc finished the last spoonful of baked beans on his plate.

"Not a security guard?" Tom asked.

"No. It's personal security for executives and also the company's R & D. The job is pretty interesting, from what they've told me."

"That's good. Hope you get it," Jim said, finishing his burger.

"As usual, we have way too much food," Kelly complained, pushing away from the table.

"I know," Gracie agreed. "Haley, don't get any ideas," she warned, eyeing the Lab's surreptitious approach to the plate laden with burgers. "You're not that sneaky. I can see you."

Chagrined, the Lab moved to where Jim sat, shoving her head under his hand.

"Yes. Yes, milady. I'll pet you again. You are very high maintenance lately," Jim jokingly protested. "Why can't you be cool like Max over there?"

Max was lying asleep under a maple near the group. He pricked up his ears briefly before resuming his nap.

"You are now her hero. After all, you furnished a great deal of cheese for her highness," Gracie joked.

"I'll never live that down." Jim stood to refill his plate. "It wasn't pretty when she plastered your parents' lawn though." He shook his head.

Momentary silence prevailed, while everyone focused on the feast of burgers, macaroni salad, and beans. Tom wiped his mouth with a paper napkin.

"Let's talk about a date for you two," Kelly insisted. "Ours is only a month away now."

Gracie smiled at Marc. His eyes crinkled in amusement, and he shook his head.

"You're not already married, are you? Tom demanded.

"No. No. It did cross my mind though. It would be so much simpler." Gracie toyed with a plastic fork. "I'm not excited about Isabelle trying to become my wedding planner, or Mom putting in her two cents. We want a simple ceremony."

"We do too," Kelly said, looking at Tom.

"And now we've got the Glen Iris booked, a harpist, and—" Tom groused,

"Slow down, my love," Kelly admonished.

Tom grimaced and rubbed his short red hair. "It's the truth. That's all I'm sayin'."

"Marc really wants to have a job in place before we set the date." Gracie reached for Marc's hand.

"Yeah. I'm a little old-fashioned, I guess. But I won't be a kept man."

"That's understandable," Jim agreed. "Give yourself some time. What's the hurry?"

Gracie looked at her business partner in surprise. They needed to have a talk and the sooner the better.

.

CHAPTER 27

The kennel was roiling with activity, between grooming appointments with Marian and Cheryl directing traffic with pick-ups and drops. The canine guests were voicing their excitement with such vitality, Gracie finally shut the door to her office. Haley and Max lounged in the backyard while she caught up on paperwork. The two dogs might as well get used to cohabitating. Marc was off to his interview with high hopes, which she prayed wouldn't be dashed.

The din increased with the opening of the door, and Jim appeared in the office, heading for the refrigerator.

"Just the man I needed to see." Gracie turned from the screen.

"That so," he answered brusquely.

"It is. We need to talk."

"All right. But it's crazy out there today."

"I know. But it's a little crazy in here."

"Meaning?" Jim asked, unscrewing the cap from a water bottle.

"I mean, I owe you an apology. I should have told you about our engagement before last night's picnic. That wasn't fair."

Jim sank into his dilapidated green-striped recliner.

"Not necessary."

"I made a mistake, and I'm sorry."

"Apology accepted then."

His icy blue eyes were hard, but Gracie also recognized the concern in them.

"I did what you told me to do in Arizona," she started. "I've dealt with Marc's job and my feelings about it. Our marriage will be different than what I had with Michael. It's okay. I'm sure my emotions will not always be in check, but nobody's perfect. Right?"

Jim arched his dark eyebrows and remained silent. He took a swig from the bottle and wiped his hand on the knee of his jeans. He certainly wasn't making this any easier.

"Jim. Let's put everything on the table. I hate feeling awkward around you."

He looked up, a half-smile softening his expression. He pushed the Yankees cap away from his forehead.

"All right, Chief. You know how I see things. I made a promise to Michael to watch out for you if anything ever happened to him. It did. I've done my best to keep that promise. If you marry Marc, I need to know that it's the right thing for you. I want you to be happy and to make certain I've fulfilled that promise."

"I know. I know. It is the right thing. I'm really sure. You've done a great job sticking with me. Supporting me in those really rough early months. We've done well together. This business is beyond what either of us imagined at the start."

"I'd have to agree. That first year was a doozy too."

"Yes, it was. We're wiser fortunately, and the business is growing. I want us to continue as business partners. Marc isn't cut out for the kennel business. He's a cop and will be in whatever form that becomes now."

"You're sure?" Jim stood, thrusting his hands into his pockets. "He understands about us?"

Gracie laughed. "He does. We talked about that a lot, as a matter of fact. You have been, are, and always will be the extra brother I apparently need. The good Lord gave me one biological sibling, but generously gave me one more who's almost tougher than the red-headed one."

"Ha! Tom needs all the help he can get. You're not an easy woman, Gracie Andersen, but I will continue our partnership until such time we decide to part ways—if ever. I've gone to the dogs with you, and now I'm officially doggone happy for you."

Gracie giggled at the bad joke, and Jim swept her up into his arms for one of his famous bear hugs.

***

Marc sat in the parking lot of DACO on the outskirts of the Batavia city limits. The job offer lay on the seat of the pickup. How would he tell Gracie about this? They'd promised to communicate clearly and often about everything. The limitation had been active cases, if he was in law enforcement. She'd readily agreed and understood why.

His mind whirled with the best approach to explain such a shift in his career path. The six-figure salary amount was dazzling, the responsibility formidable, but a challenge he welcomed. Max could partner with him and they'd both receive more training. Unfortunately, secrecy was paramount, there was a great deal of travel, and a security clearance from the U.S. government was required. His family situation with a half-brother sitting in federal prison might be an obstacle to obtain the clearance, but the defense company hadn't hesitated in handing him the generous proposal.

It was the opportunity of a lifetime. Fingering the textured letterhead, he refolded it, and slid the offer into the inside pocket of his suitcoat.

Thank you for taking the time to read Washed Up, the fourth book in the Gracie Andersen Mystery Series. If you enjoyed it, please consider telling your friends or posting a short review. Word of mouth is an author's best friend and much appreciated. Thank you. –Laurinda Wallace

ABOUT THE AUTHOR

Laurinda Wallace lives in the beautiful high desert of southeast Arizona where she and her husband enjoy hiking and exploring. A lifelong bookworm and writer, she loves writing about her hometown area and the West.

Want to know more? Visit **www.laurindawallace.com** for more information and be sure to sign up for her newsletter. Subscribers receive exclusive discounts and insider book news. Your email is never shared or sold.

BOOKS BY LAURINDA WALLACE

The Gracie Andersen Mysteries

Family Matters

By the Book

Fly By Night

Washed Up

Pins & Needles

The Mistletoe Murders

True-Crime Memoir

Too Close to Home: The Samantha Zaldivar Case

Inspirational

The Time Under Heaven

Gardens of the Heart

Historical Fiction Short Story

The Murder of Alfred Silverheels

Historical Mystery

The Disappearance of Sara Colter

Made in the USA
Las Vegas, NV
07 March 2022

45179098R00085